H

Key Point

Basic concepts in point form.

Close Up

Additional hints, notes, tips or background information.

Watch Out!

Areas where problems frequently occur.

Quick Tip

Concise ideas to help you learn what you need to know.

Remember This!

Essential material for mastery of the topic.

COLES NOTES

Moms and Dads' Guide to . . .

Helping Your Child With Math

Key ideas by topic

for grades 1 to 8

With activities &

brain teasers

ABOUT COLES NOTES

COLES NOTES have been an indispensable aid to students on five continents since 1948.

COLES NOTES now offer titles on a wide range of general interest topics as well as traditional academic subject areas and individual literary works. All COLES NOTES are written by experts in their fields and reviewed for accuracy by independent authorities and the Coles Editorial Board.

COLES NOTES provide clear, concise explanations of their subject areas. Proper use of COLES NOTES will result in a broader understanding of the topic being studied. For academic subjects, COLES NOTES are an invaluable aid for study, review and exam preparation. For literary works, COLES NOTES provide interesting interpretations and evaluations which supplement the text but are not intended as a substitute for reading the text itself. Use of the NOTES will serve not only to clarify the material being studied, but should enhance the reader's enjoyment of the topic.

COLES PUBLISHING. A division of Prospero Books

Toronto - Canada

Printed in Canada

Cataloguing in Publication Data

Erdman, Wayne, 1954-

Moms and dads' guide to ... helping your child with math :
key ideas, by topic, for grades 1 to 8, with activities and brain teasers

(Coles notes) ISBN 0-7740-0598-X

1. Mathematics—Study and teaching (Elementary).
2. Education—Parent participaton. I. Title. II. Series

QA135.5.E72 1999 372.7 C99-931034-8

Publisher: Nigel Berrisford

Editing: Paul Kropp Communications

Book design: Karen Petherick, Markham, Ontario

Layout: Sun Ngo

Manufactured by Webcom Limited

Cover finish: Webcom's Exclusive DURACOAT

Contents

Introduction 1

Chapter 1 **The home environment** 3
A place to study
Motivation
Creating a schedule
Friend, family or tutor

Chapter 2 **Basic operations in math (Grades 2-5)** 9
Simple adding and subtracting
Addition with carrying
Simple multiplication and division
Multiplication with larger numbers
Long division

Chapter 3 **Positive and negative numbers (integers) (Grades 6-7)** 17
Adding integers
Subtracting integers
Multiplying and dividing integers

Chapter 4 **Fractions and decimals (Grades 3-8)** 22
What is a fraction?
Equivalent fractions
Adding and subtracting fractions
Multiplying fractions
Dividing fractions
Converting fractions to decimals
Adding and subtracting decimals
Multiplying decimals
Dividing decimals

Chapter 5 **Helping with percents (Grades 6-7)** 33
The concept of a percent
Working with percents

Chapter 6 **Helping with measurement (Grades 2-7)** 37
Beginning metric measurement
Metric conversions
Circumference of a circle
Concept of area
Area of a rectangle
Capacity of containers
Volumes of solids

Money concepts
Reading and estimating time

Chapter 7 **Statistics: Venn diagrams, collecting data, graphs and averages (Grades 2-7)** 45
Classifying with Venn diagrams
Collecting and organizing data
Collecting, organizing and interpreting data
Line and circle graphs
Measuring "averages": mean, median, mode

Chapter 8 **Helping with chance (Grades 2-7)** 53
Understanding chance
Calculating probabilities
Calculating theoretical probabilities

Chapter 9 **Helping with geometry (Grades 3-7)** 58
Working with two-dimensional shapes
Understanding cubes and other solids
Building solids from nets
Sketching three-dimensional solids
Measuring angles with protractors
Angles and parallel lines

Chapter 10 **Graphing and transformations (Grades 2-7)** 64
Understanding a coordinate grid
Using a coordinate grid
Understanding symmetry
Slides (translations) on a grid
Flips (reflections) and turns (rotations)
Tilings (tessellations)

Chapter 11 **Helping with introductory algebra (Grades 5-7)** 69
Patterns
Graphs of relations
The concept of a variable
Solving simple equations

Chapter 12 **Some tips on . . .** 76
Mathematics software
Mathematics workbooks
Games that build math skills

Chapter 13 **Ten math puzzlers** 84

Chapter 14 **Five math games for the family** 89

Appendix **What your child should know, by grade level** 92

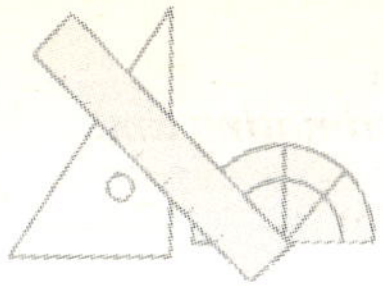

Introduction

Children regularly ask, "Why do we have to learn math?" Their frustration comes from a lack of understanding of basic mathematical ideas and because they have trouble seeing the applications surrounding these concepts. Many people, including some parents, feel that today's math is confusing or unnecessary. But that belief could not be further from the truth. Mathematics is everywhere. We see it on the bus, at home, in the workplace, in newspapers and at play - we just don't recognize it. Our children need math so that they can understand and work with numbers and shapes, work with technology, develop problem-solving strategies and improve their logical thinking. Perhaps most important is that math helps children develop from concrete to abstract thinkers - important in everything from computers to business.

All too often, parents are overheard saying, "I was lousy at math too, so it's okay." Unfortunately, it's not okay. It is as important for our children to be numerate as it is to be literate. Parents can help by making math important to both themselves and their children. Help your children see the math around them. Make real-life math interesting and fun. Explain and show how math can help solve problems involving measurement (e.g., science), calculations (e.g., cooking), chance (e.g., games), geometry (e.g., building), patterns (e.g., art), percents (e.g., shopping), statistics (e.g., sports), etc.

The goals of this book are to help parents understand how to help their children in math, to interest both parents and kids in mathematics and to show techniques of making math more understandable and easier to learn. We will use concrete examples and activities, to provide insight into how math is taught in our elementary schools and to indicate the mathematical concepts your child should know by each grade level from grade 3 to 7.

Use this book to help your children when they are having difficulty, when the concepts they bring home do not seem clear. As well, this is an idea book for family activities and a quick reference for your child's elementary-school math curriculum. Keep in mind that math topics are rarely taught in isolation in schools. Math is taught in context, as it relates to the world around us. Problem solving is a regular part of the process. It is taught as a skill rather than being tacked onto the end of each unit. This book incorporates this modern approach into the activities, but emphasises the basic skills in each mathematical area. Obviously, the whole elementary-school curriculum can not be covered in a single book. The topics chosen represent those areas of math that children find most difficult or that require more parental guidance to develop a strong foundation in mathematics.

CHAPTER ONE

The home environment

Your home environment is where any discussion on homework should begin. What kind of place does your child have in which to study? What kind of support is offered by you and the rest of the family? Is it positive, or is it a constant battle to get your child to start her homework? What kind of schedule does she have? Is it structured? Are there too many distractions? Until these issues are settled, no "help" book is going to be of much help.

A PLACE TO STUDY

By the time your child is receiving homework regularly, she should have a permanent place to do work. In order to do homework properly, a child must have a quiet place where she can be alone and concentrate. The kitchen table or her own desk are usually the best places, so she can be left undisturbed when working, but is close enough for you to be available to help. Guide her to the best places to do her homework, but let her make the final decision.

Some of the worst places are in front of the television, near a telephone, or near a playroom or any place that will distract your child and divert her attention from her homework. The study area need not be large, but should still provide enough room to spread out a few books, papers and supplies. It is extremely important that the space be well lit to reduce eye fatigue.

It is equally important that your child have her own set of supplies:

pencils	pencil crayons	pens	markers	scissors

stickers	math set	dictionary	stapler	eraser

glue	lined and graph paper	pencil sharpener	correction fluid	calculator

If the study space is her own desk, one drawer can be set aside for pencils, pens, etc., another for paper. If your child's study space is in the kitchen or another multi-use space, sealable containers are ideal for holding supplies. Keeping the study space organized and tidying after the homework is complete teaches good organizational skills and shortens the daily set-up time.

WHEN SHOULD WE BUY A COMPUTER?

Computers are now being used in virtually all schools across Canada. They are used for doing research, typing assignments, compiling and displaying data, etc. Your children will be at an advantage if you have one at home by about grade 4. They are essential by high school. Buy the most powerful and up-to-date computer you can afford. See chapter 12 for tips on buying software.

MOTIVATION

How you relate to your child plays an important role in his intellectual development, self-esteem and achievement. Providing regular encouragement and support shows that you are on his side and that you care. Consider these examples of supportive and non-supportive comments:

"Can you show me what you did in school today? Maybe I can help you get started on your homework."

"Sit down and do your homework right now!"

"I see you had some trouble on that test. Let's look at it and try to understand where you went wrong."

"You failed that test! Didn't you study? No more TV until you get your grades up."

"Good! You got seven questions right this time. That's one better than last time."

"How come you got three wrong on this quiz? What's wrong with you?"

A child usually works well and develops good study habits if you are part of the process. Helping him get started or do unfamiliar or difficult work goes a long way in building an independent learner. When your child brings home a low mark on a test or assignment, give positive encouragement. Remember, it is just one mark. Ask him what he had trouble with and whether he knows how to fix the errors. And by all means, praise him when he brings home top marks or even an improved mark over the previous one.

Give your child rewards. Stickers or treats for homework completion, good marks, improvement in marks and neatness are excellent motivators.

CREATING A SCHEDULE

Children need organization and structure. Schedules and test-planning sheets help kids organize their time and keep them focused. Homework is best done shortly after school, when the information is fresh in their minds. A short break for playtime or to watch a favorite TV show is okay, but get them started early, before dinner, if possible.

Children respond well to a schedule. Make up a weekly calendar. Include all music lessons, sports activities, important events, tests and assignments. Fit in leisure and homework time. Scheduling homework at a regular time may help keep your child organized. She will respond best to a consistent scheduling of her activities. However, allowing her to develop her own schedule helps develop a sense of autonomy and responsibility. Know your child's attention span. Which would be better - one half-hour session or two 15-minute sessions? Pay attention to changes in mood and energy and be flexible.

Example of a weekly schedule

	SUNDAY	MONDAY	TUESDAY	WEDNESDAY	THURSDAY	FRIDAY	SATURDAY
Due at school:			Dividing test			Geometry assign.	
4:00	Hockey	TV	Homework	Hockey	TV	TV	
5:00		Homework	Piano lessons	Homework	Homework	Homework	Piano practice
6:00	Dinner	Dinner	Dinner	Dinner	Dinner	Dinner	Dinner
7:00	Homework	Homework	Homework	Homework	Homework	Homework	
8:00	TV	TV	Hockey	TV	TV	TV	
9:00	Piano practice	Piano practice		Piano practice	Piano practice	Piano practice	

If your child is having difficulty planning her study times for tests or completing her assignments on time, student planners or study-planning sheets are ideal. Many schools now give out or sell student planners to the kids in the middle grades and beyond. Study-planning sheets help your child plan the tasks needed to complete the assignment or study schedule. They keep her focused on the activities and on the order in which they need to be done. Make sure your child speaks to the teacher and completes the necessary information when the test or assignment is announced. Work with her to plan her schedule, making sure it is detailed and contains the appropriate activities needed to complete her assignment or studying.

Example of a study planning sheet

TOPIC: Test on area of squares, rectangles and triangles	**DATE DUE:** Oct. 15
DATE	**ACTIVITY**
Oct. 10	Page 34 #6, 7, 8
Oct. 11	Page 37 #1-10
Oct. 12	Worksheet on area of a triangle
Oct. 13	Review ex page 40 and study
Oct. 14	Study squares, triangles & rectangles (1 hour)
Oct. 15	Test

FRIEND, FAMILY OR TUTOR?

Parents regularly wonder who should help their child with his homework. As a parent, it is paramount that you take an active role in helping him understand and complete his homework. However, children frequently need help in the form of clarification of notes, ideas and assignments. At that point, he should contact a classmate who would understand the day's assignment. Ongoing periodic help, though, should be given by *you*. If there is a topic you do not understand, make this an opportunity to learn it yourself. Older brothers and sisters are a goldmine of help, especially if your children get along well.

If your child is struggling a great deal and does not respond to your help or you cannot provide the time needed, consider a paid tutor. Contact the school for in-school resources. Your child's teacher may offer after-school help. If your child is a special-ed student, extra help is readily available in the resource room. The librarian is another source of help, too.

The school will have names of older students who may be available to tutor. Children of friends and neighbors may be available to tutor as well. Professional tutoring agencies are expensive and may not be prepared to tutor an elementary-school student, but consider them as well. Once you find a tutor, hire her on a trial basis, until you see if she gets along with your child, and has an appropriate style and manner with him.

A good tutor will:

- engage your child in dialogue, asking him to explain what he *can* do along with what he cannot do
- go over tests and assignments with your child to determine where he is struggling
- explain concepts in appropriate language and give numerous examples
- use concrete examples to explain abstract concepts (e.g., two sets of 10 playing cards makes 20 cards, which means that $2 \times 10 = 20$)
- provide additional work for your child, containing a variety of exercises
- keep the tutoring sessions to less than one hour. A half hour is best
- offer encouragement, encouragement, encouragement

Remember, if your child is struggling, getting an A should not be the goal. Comprehension and increased confidence are the most important first steps.

CHAPTER TWO

Basic operations in math
(Grades 2-5)

SIMPLE ADDING AND SUBTRACTING (GRADE 2-3)

Your child should have had a great deal of exposure to these facts in early grades. Nevertheless, some children may still have difficulty with these concepts. Accuracy and quick recall should be stressed.

Activity 1

If, for example, your child is still adding by counting (on fingers or out loud), review the concepts by using what are known as ten-cards. These are cards that are 5 squares by 2 squares. A certain number of squares are filled with a dot, a star or a sticker to represent a given 1-digit number. Regular use allows your child to build a number image and is very helpful in understanding addition and subtraction facts.

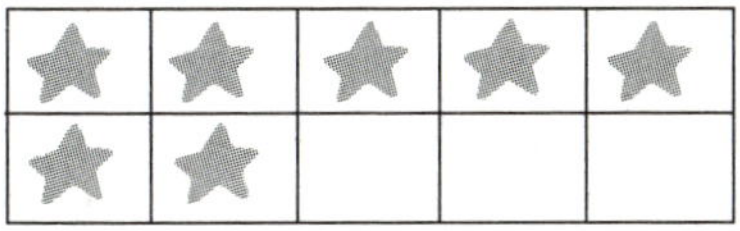

This ten-card represents the number 7. It can be used for the following types of questions:

- How many squares are filled if we add 2 to 7?
- How many squares would be filled if we subtract 3?
- Name pairs of numbers that add to give 7.

If the sum exceeds 10, continue on a second ten-card. The filled card would then represent the tens digit of a 2-digit number.

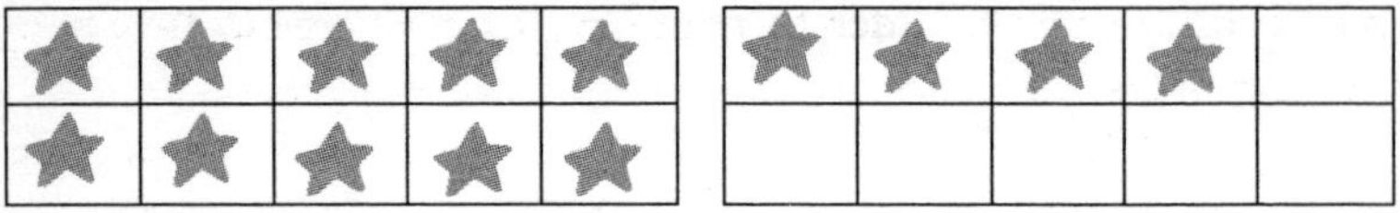

This pair of ten-cards represents the number 14. They could also represent 10+4, 9+5, 20−6, or a host of other addition and subtraction facts.

Activity 2

Flash cards are a traditional way of practicing the basic skills. By their nature, the teacher or parent sits opposite the child as an authority.

Using skills triangles invites you to sit beside your child in a more helpful manner. Have your child make a number of triangles about 8 cm (3 in.) wide. Place two numbers in the bottom corners and their sum in the top corner.

The triangle shown below illustrates the sum 7+8=15.

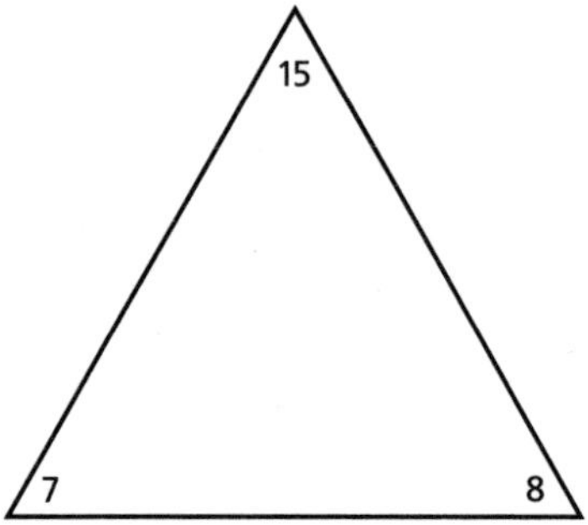

When you are writing the numbers on the triangles, ask your child what these numbers represent. Then encourage him to write them on the triangles himself. Once complete, cover up the number in the top corner and ask your child for the sum of the two numbers. If he gets it correct, go on to the next triangle. If he is incorrect, ask him to try *one more time*. After that, more attempts are counterproductive. Next, cover up one of the bottom numbers and ask him to subtract. Eventually, the activity should include both addition and subtraction mixed together. They should always be practiced together in order to reinforce the relationship between the operations.

ADDITION WITH CARRYING (GRADE 3)

As soon as your child has mastered his basic skills, he is ready to move on to 2- and 3-digit numbers with regrouping. Children frequently make errors by placing the carried digit in the space for the answer instead of in the next column - or they forget about it completely. The most frequent error, however, is not aligning the digits in the proper column.

Activity 3

To overcome all of these errors, give your child some grid paper. Have him line up the digits along the units column, one square per digit. When adding, place the carried digit above the new column, because it now represents 10 or 100, etc. When subtracting, cross out the borrowed digit and place the new one above it. Place the borrowed digit beside the appropriate digit. In the examples below, regrouping with 237+48 and 93−27 are shown.

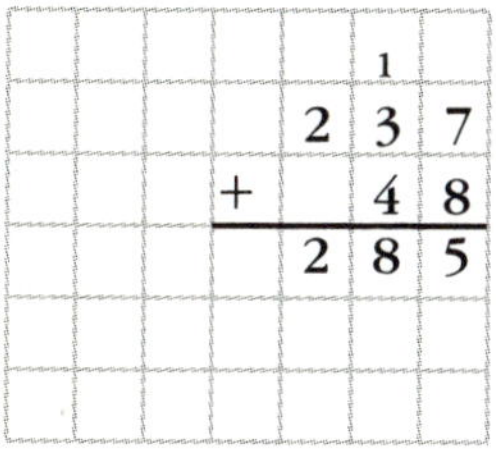

Even though you are regrouping 10, fewer errors are made by carrying just the 1.

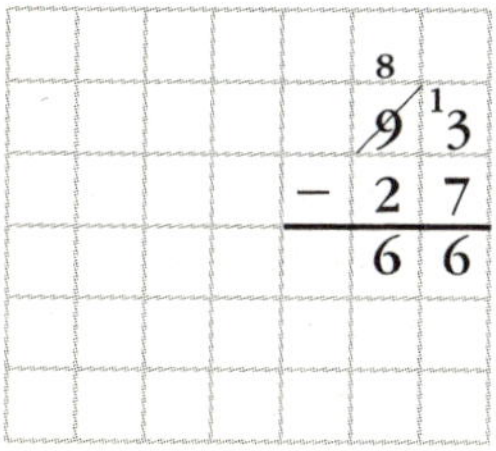

Writing down the borrowed digit helps to reduce errors with subtraction facts.

When you check your child's homework, double check to see that he follows these guidelines.

Activity 4

Use an old calendar to find addition and subtraction patterns. Any month will do.

SUN	MON	TUE	WED	THU	FRI	SAT
		1	2	3	4	5
6	7	8	9	10	11	12
13	14	15	16	17	18	19
20	21	22	23	24	25	26
27	28	29	30	31		

Draw a square around any 4 of the dates as shown. Add the numbers along each diagonal.

$4+12=16$
$5+11=16$
and
$7+15=22$
$8+14=22$

What pattern do you see? Check to see if this is true with other months.

SUN	MON	TUE	WED	THU	FRI	SAT
		1	2	3	4	5
6	7	8	9	10	11	12
13	14	15	16	17	18	19
20	21	22	23	24	25	26
27	28	29	30	31		

Draw a square around any 9 of the dates as shown.

Look for an addition pattern.
Look for a subtraction pattern.

Check your patterns with another square and then on another calendar.

Make up some questions and challenge your friends, your teacher and your parents.

SIMPLE MULTIPLICATION AND DIVISION (GRADE 3-4)

Multiplication is best learned by treating it as repeated addition. Sometimes you can help understanding by investigating patterns. Division facts should be learned alongside multiplication. Many children find division skills more difficult to master. However, some children find them easier because, they say, "the answer is already provided." This is true if they have mastered their multiplication facts.

Activity 5

To develop the concept of multiplication, show it as repeated addition, by using pictures or symbols.

Show how 3 groups of 5 pencils gives 15 pencils.

$3 \times 5 = 15$

Have your child illustrate multiplication of two 2-digit numbers up to 5×5.

Division concepts can be developed in the same way, being shown as sharing. Fifteen pencils can be divided into 3 groups of 5 pencils.

Activity 6

To reinforce these concepts, use a grid. Draw rectangles with dimensions of up to 9 by 9. The number of small squares will be the resulting product when the dimensions are multiplied together

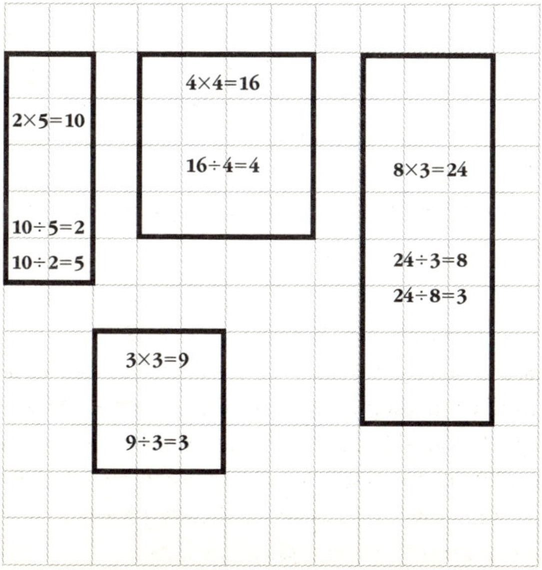

Make sure the division facts are included on the grid so that both multiplication and division facts are reinforced.

Activity 7
To provide drill in multiplication and division facts, use the skills triangle as shown in Activity 2.

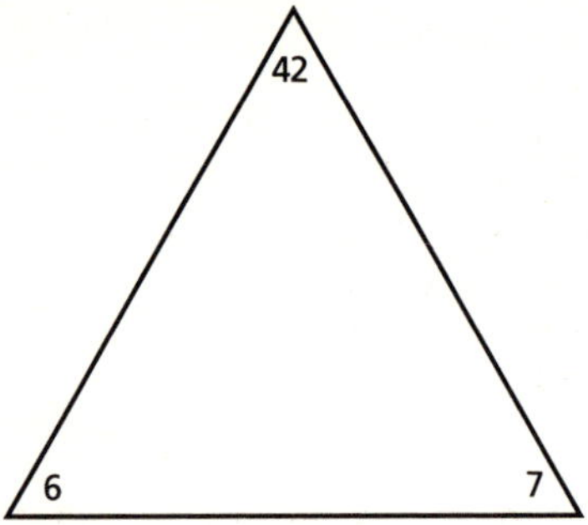

This time, cover the top number for multiplication or one of the lower numbers for division. The triangle above represents $6 \times 7 = 42$, $42 \div 6 = 7$ and $42 \div 7 = 6$.

MULTIPLICATION WITH LARGER NUMBERS (GRADE 4-5)

Activity 8
When multiplying larger numbers, the concept of regrouping (carrying) needs to be developed. This is done by first considering the larger number in expanded form.

For example, when multiplying 6×27, think of it as $6 \times 7 + 6 \times 20$:

$$\begin{array}{rl} 27 & \\ \underline{\times 6} & \\ 42 & \leftarrow 6 \times 7 \\ \underline{120} & \leftarrow 6 \times 20 \\ 162 & \end{array}$$

Do a few more examples such as this before processing to the traditional method of regrouping:

$$\begin{array}{rl} 27 & \\ \underline{\times 6} & \\ 162 & \leftarrow 6 \times 7 = 42\text{, regrouping the 4} \\ & \quad\text{and add it to } 6 \times 2 = 12 \end{array}$$

Activity 9

Eventually, your child will progress to multiplying when both numbers are two or more digits. As in Activity 8, begin by multiplying in expanded form:

$$
\begin{array}{rl}
63 & \\
\times\ 24 & \\
\hline
12 & \leftarrow\ \ 4\times3 \\
240 & \leftarrow\ \ 4\times60 \\
60 & \leftarrow 20\times3 \\
1200 & \leftarrow 20\times60 \\
\hline
1512 &
\end{array}
$$

Progress to the traditional method of multiplying by regrouping. Writing down the regrouped digit or even using fingers as holders works well. Using zeroes to fill the unused places in the second and further rows, helps to align the digits properly. Using a grid helps too.

$$
\begin{array}{rl}
63 & \\
\times\ 24 & \\
\hline
252 & \leftarrow 4\times3=12\text{, regroup the 1; }4\times6=24\text{ and add 1 to get 25.} \\
1260 & \leftarrow \text{Place a zero in the units column first. Then multiply} \\
\hline
1512 & \ \ \ \text{by 2.}
\end{array}
$$

LONG DIVISION (GRADE 4-5)

This is the final "basic skill" involving whole numbers. Children find the procedure relatively easy to follow, but often miss steps or misalign the columns.

When helping your child, make sure he understands the vocabulary and standard forms:

dividend ÷ divisor = quotient

$$\begin{array}{r} \textit{quotient} \\ \textit{divisor}\overline{\smash{)}\textit{dividend}} \end{array}$$

Children often reverse the divisor and dividend. Check to make sure your child has not done this.

Activity 10

To help your child in the initial stages (answers without remainders) follow the procedure below, filling in with zeroes as shown:

		1	4	
	6)	8	4	
		6	0	
		2	4	
		2	4	
			0	

← Inititially, divide 6 into 8.

← Children understand that they are multiplying by 10, not 1, so fill in with a zero.

Make sure your child checks by multiplying $6 \times 14 = 84$ to see if he divided correctly.

Activity 11

When dividing larger numbers or numbers with remainders, use the same development before using shortcuts.

		1	3	R4
	7)	9	5	
		7	0	
		2	5	
		2	1	
			4	

When designing questions for your child, always start with dividends whose first digit is less than the divisor. In other words, give your child $95 \div 7$ before $65 \div 7$. This way, the blank space above the first digit of the dividend can be treated as the next stage in your child's development.

		X	9	R2
	7)	6	5	
		6	3	
			2	

It may help to insert an X in the first position, so your child is not tempted to place the 9 there.

CHAPTER THREE

Positive and negative numbers (integers)

(Grades 6-7)

Even though it is not taught until grade 6 or 7, children understand the concept of integers at a much earlier age. Positive and negative temperature and profit and loss are two examples. Integers are simply the positive and negative counting numbers, plus zero. Stay away from raised signs (e.g., $^{-}3$ or $^{+}5$ were frequently used in the past). Current practice is to place the sign immediately to the left of the number (-3 or $+5$). Where children experience difficulty is with the four basic operations. They tend to memorize rules instead of understanding the concepts. The following exercises will help.

ADDING INTEGERS (GRADE 6-7)

Activity 1

An easy way of teaching operations with integers is to use integer chips. Two different-colored poker chips or cardboard squares work well.

 represents positive 1  represents negative 1

The first step is to understand the concept of zero. Any equal number of positive and negative chips equals zero.

 $2+(-2)=0$

 $3+(-3)=0$

An imbalance is how positive or negative sums are created.
To create and evaluate $(-3)+5$, use 3 negative and 5 positive chips:

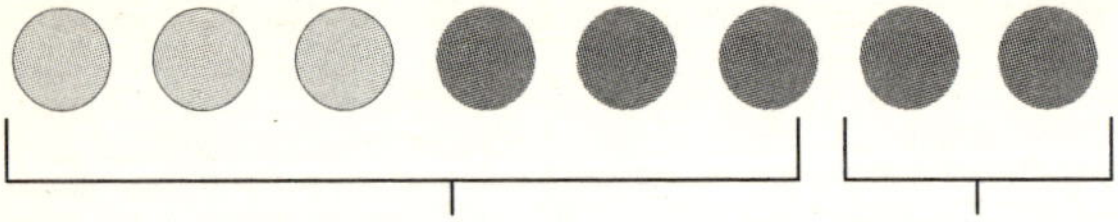

For $4+(-7)$, use 4 positive and 7 negative chips:

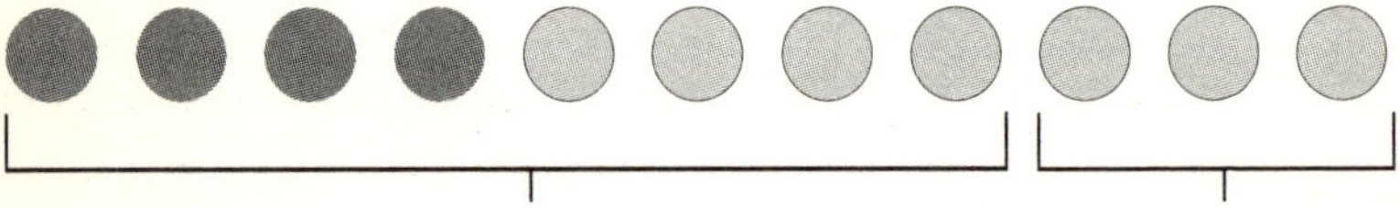

For $(-3)+(-2)$, use 3 negative and 2 more negative chips:

No cancelling out because no 0 is produced.
Therefore, $(-3)+(-2)=-5$

The following addition rules can now be developed:

Positive + Positive = Positive
Negative + Negative = Negative
Positive + Negative → Subtract as with whole numbers and take the sign of the bigger number.

SUBTRACTING INTEGERS (GRADE 6-7)

Activity 2

Use the integer chips as in Activity 1. Your child needs to understand subtraction as taking away or removing.

Showing $7-3$ is straightforward:

Start with 7 chips. Removing 3 leaves 4: $7-3=4$

To show $7-(-3)$ requires creating a form of zero:

Starting with 7 posititve chips, there are no negative chips to take away. To overcome that, add a form of zero, 3 positive and 3 negative chips.

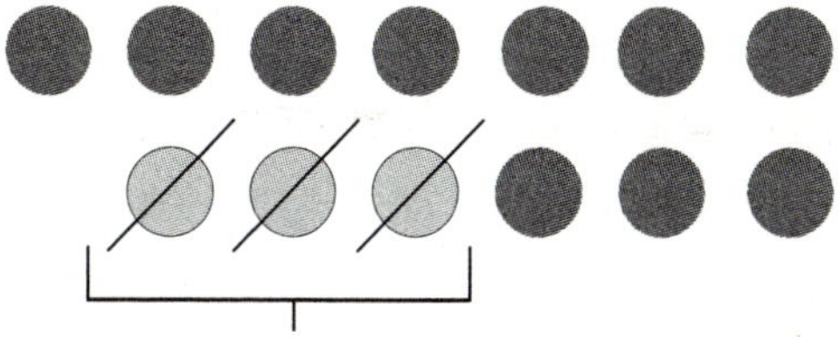

Then take 3 negative chips away so that $7-(-3)=10$.

As long as you are able to "create zero," any subtraction of two integers can be illustrated with integer chips. Try about 10 of these, writing down the results each time.

Careful observation of the results and comparison of the results from addition should help in understanding that ***to subtract integers, add the opposite sign of the number following the subtraction sign***.

For example: $2-5=2+(-5)$
$=-3$

$7-(-3)=7+(+3)$
$=10$

$(-4)-(+5)=(-4)+(-5)$
$=-9$

MULTIPLYING AND DIVIDING INTEGERS (GRADE 6-7)

Activity 3

Using integer chips, this can be done in the same way multiplication was developed in Activities 5 and 6.

Show multiplication as collecting sets of negatives and division as the opposite of multiplication.

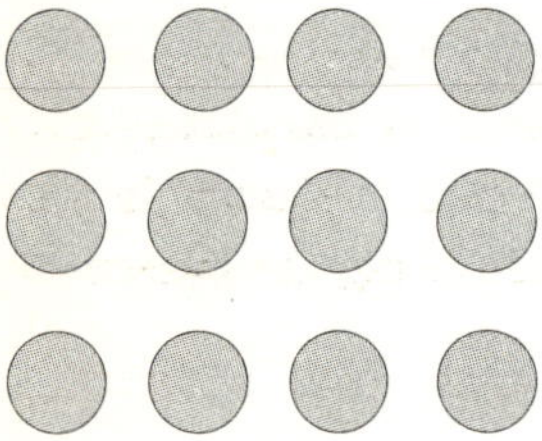

3 sets of 4 chips
$3\times(-4)=-12$

As division is the opposite of multiplication, we can see that $-12\div4=-3$ and $-12\div(-3)=4$

To illustrate $(-2)\times(-3)$, we again need to create zero. This time, we need to remove 2 sets of 3 negatives, we create zero twice, each with 3 positives and 3 negatives:

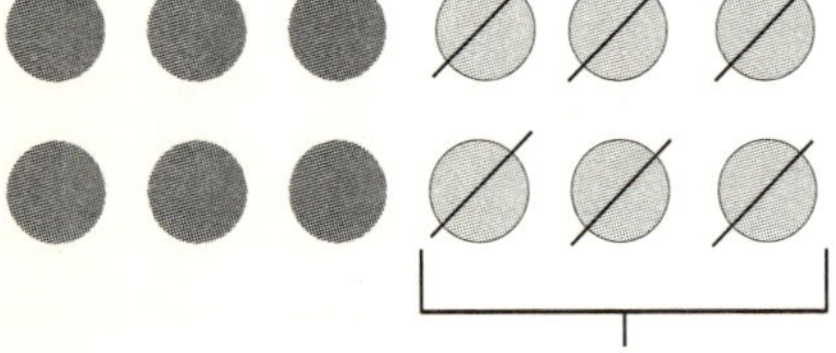

Removing 2 sets of -3 leaves us with $+6$.
Multiplication: $(-2)\times(-3)=6$
Division: $6\div(-2)=-3$
$6\div(-3)=-2$

Careful observation allows us to develop rules for multiplication and division of integers:

Positive × Positive = Positive
Negative × Negative = Positive
Negative × Positive = Negative
Positive × Negative = Negative

Positive ÷ Positive = Positive
Negative ÷ Negative = Positive
Negative ÷ Positive = Negative
Positive ÷ Negative = Negative

Allow your child to use the chips until she is very comfortable with them. There is no need to be concerned about relying on them. She will give them up when she is ready. Once your child understands the concepts, the rules will make more sense. At that point, plenty of practice is important. Check for the correct signs in her answers. If necessary, you may need to re-explain using the integer chips.

CHAPTER FOUR

Fractions and decimals

(Grades 3-8)

Children often have difficulties with fractions and decimals because they are new concepts and are fairly abstract. Making them concrete is the key to helping your child. Your examples should always be with pictures or objects that can be manipulated.

WHAT IS A FRACTION? (GRADE 3)

Activity 1

Your child needs to understand that a fraction is a part of a whole. For that reason, draw diagrams that illustrate this idea.

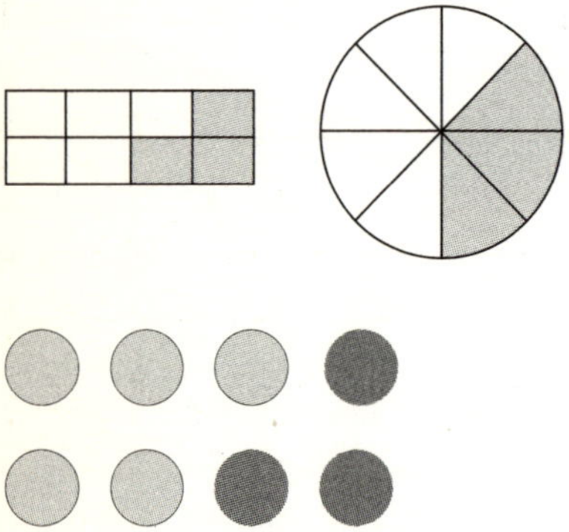

These first two diagrams show $\frac{3}{8}$ of a whole and are preferable to the third diagram that shows $\frac{3}{8}$ of a set.

Draw some diagrams and have him shade in various fractions. Keep them simple, up to tenths.

Activity 2

Use food such as pizza, chocolate bars, pies, cookies, etc. Stress the concept that the parts are equal parts, or they are not fractions.

Make sure you explain that the top number is the number of pieces you eat (shaded ones) and the bottom number is the total number of pieces into which you cut the pizza.

Activity 3

Paper folding helps some kids understand the difference between sixths and eighths. Have him fold a sheet of paper in half. Fold it in half again and again. This will result in eighths. Then ask him to fold a new sheet of paper so it results in sixths or twelfths. This same concept can also be illustrated by slicing a pie in half, then into eighths or sixths. In addition to improving the concept of fractions, this activity helps to improve problem-solving skills.

EQUIVALENT FRACTIONS (GRADE 4–6)

Activity 4

To illustrate the equivalency of fractions, have your child cut 7 strips of graph paper so each is 12 squares long. He should then divide the strips into 1, 2, 3, 4, 6, 8 and 12 parts, labelling each part appropriately. Ask him to find as many sets of equivalent fractions as he can.

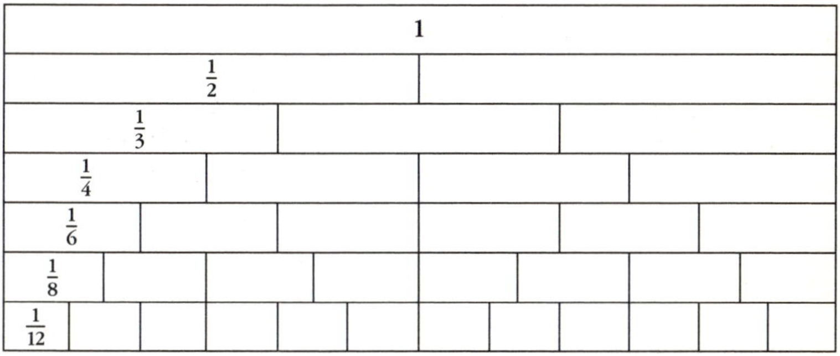

Some equivalent fractions he should be able to find:

$$\frac{1}{2}=\frac{2}{4}=\frac{3}{6}=\frac{4}{8}=\frac{6}{12}$$

$$\frac{1}{3}=\frac{2}{6}=\frac{4}{12}$$

$$\frac{1}{4}=\frac{2}{8}=\frac{3}{12}$$

Next, show him how multiplying or dividing both the numerator and denominator by the same number (or factor) always results in an equivalent fraction. Follow that up by giving him a pencil-and-paper exercise in finding equivalent fractions by the common denominator (multiplying or dividing) method (Activity 5).

Activity 5

To illustrate relative sizes and the ranking of fractions, use the strips shown in Activity 3. Visually, your child can see that $\frac{2}{3}$ is less than $\frac{3}{4}$. However, your child needs to progress to finding the **common denominator** as the preferred, and faster, method of comparing and ranking fractions: if the denominators are the same, it allows for an easy comparison of the number of "pizza slices" eaten (numerator).

To compare $\frac{2}{3}$ and $\frac{3}{4}$, first find the lowest common multiple of 3 and 4: $3 \times 4 = 12$.

Now, multiply each numerator by the same number as in the denominator:

$$\frac{2 \times 4}{3 \times 4} = \frac{8}{12} \quad \text{and} \quad \frac{3 \times 3}{4 \times 3} = \frac{9}{12}$$

$$\frac{8}{12} < \frac{9}{12}$$

$$\text{Therefore,} \quad \frac{2}{3} < \frac{3}{4}$$

Note:
< means "is less than."
> means "is greater than."
The symbol opens up to the greater number.

Follow this up by giving your child a worksheet of comparing simple fractions.

ADDING AND SUBTRACTING FRACTIONS (GRADE 7-8)

Adding and subtracting fractions is not very different from working with whole numbers. Adding and subtracting should be taught or reviewed together. Children frequently experience difficulties with denominators (bottom). They tend to add them or simply ignore them, instead of keeping them the same. This is because they do not understand that, by adding or subtracting fractions, they are simply "collecting" the parts. By collecting them, the parts (denominators) do not change, the number collected (numerators) does.

Activity 6

To illustrate addition of fractions with the same denominator, draw an 8 by 1 grid on a sheet of paper. There will be 8 squares, each representing a fraction of $\frac{1}{8}$. Shade in 3 of them. Then shade in a further 2 of them to represent addition of fractions.

$$\frac{3}{8}+\frac{2}{8}=\frac{5}{8}$$

This can be done with various size grids and will help your child understand how to add or subtract fractions with the same denominator.

Activity 7

To demonstrate adding fractions with unlike denominators, make strips, similar to those in Activity 3, showing $\frac{1}{3}$ and $\frac{1}{4}$. Then, lay the strips side-by-side on a twelfths strip. They will cover 7 squares, or 7 twelfths.

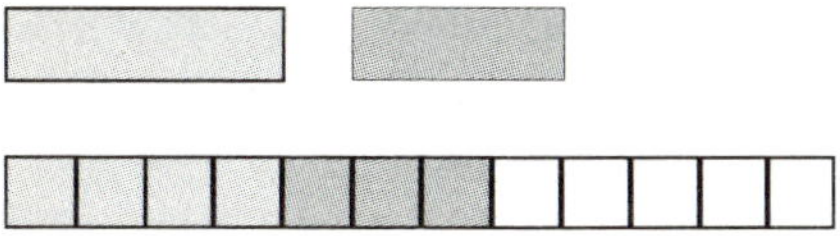

$$\frac{1}{3}+\frac{1}{4}=\,?$$

$$\frac{4}{12}+\frac{3}{12}=\frac{7}{12}$$

Your child needs to progress to finding the common denominator (Activity 4) before adding or subtracting.

$$\begin{aligned}\frac{1}{3}+\frac{1}{4}&=\frac{1\times4}{3\times4}+\frac{1\times3}{4\times3}\\&=\frac{4}{12}+\frac{3}{12}\\&=\frac{7}{12}\end{aligned}$$

$$\begin{aligned}\frac{5}{6}-\frac{2}{5}&=\frac{5\times5}{6\times5}-\frac{2\times6}{5\times6}\\&=\frac{25}{30}-\frac{12}{30}\\&=\frac{13}{30}\end{aligned}$$

At this point, restrict your exercises to single-digit denominators. This topic requires a great deal of practice. Provide your child with plenty of help and opportunities to succeed.

Activity 8

For real-life contexts for adding and subtracting fractions, make up examples with pizzas, cakes, etc. Here is one example:

Barb ate $\frac{1}{4}$ of a pizza and Sarah ate $\frac{3}{8}$ of it. What fraction of the pizza did they eat?

$$\frac{1}{4}+\frac{3}{8}=\frac{2}{8}+\frac{3}{8}$$

$$=\frac{5}{8}$$

They ate $\frac{5}{8}$ of the pizza.

MULTIPLYING FRACTIONS (GRADE 7-8)

Most children understand that half of a half is a quarter, based on their own experience with such things as money. You can use this concept when helping your child with multiplying fractions. In math, the word "of" generally means multiplication.

Activity 9

To show how to multiply $\frac{1}{2}\times\frac{1}{3}$ (or any pair of fractions), show $\frac{1}{3}$ in a diagram. Then cut each segment in half. There are now 6 segments, showing that $\frac{1}{2}$ of $\frac{1}{3}$ is $\frac{1}{6}$.

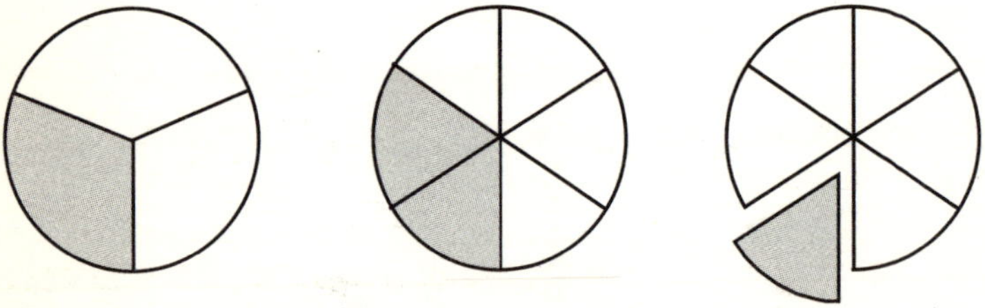

$\frac{1}{3}$ $\qquad$ $\frac{1}{2}$ of each third $\qquad$ $\frac{1}{2}\times\frac{1}{3}$

$$=\frac{1\times1}{2\times3}=\frac{1}{6}$$

This should help your child understand that, when multiplying fractions, you simply multiply the numerators and denominators separately. At this point, you can make up a practice worksheet for your child. For example, fill a page with exercises such as:

(a) $\frac{2}{3} \times \frac{1}{5} =$ (b) $\frac{5}{7} \times \frac{3}{8} =$ (c) $\frac{2}{9} \times \frac{4}{5} =$

Three common mistakes kids make are

- multiplying only the numerators or denominators
- cross multiplying the numerators and denominators
- finding the common denominator before multiplying

When your child is doing his homework, have him check for these errors in particular.

DIVIDING FRACTIONS (GRADE 7-8)

All too often, children can recite a rule for dividing fractions, but fail to apply the rule properly. They need to understand that, just as with whole numbers, division means dividing up into equal groups.

Activity 10

$6 \div 2$ means, how many double groups are in 6? Answer: 3
$6 \div \frac{1}{2}$ means, how many half groups are in 6? Answer: 12

This could also mean, how many half-doughnuts are in 6 doughnuts?

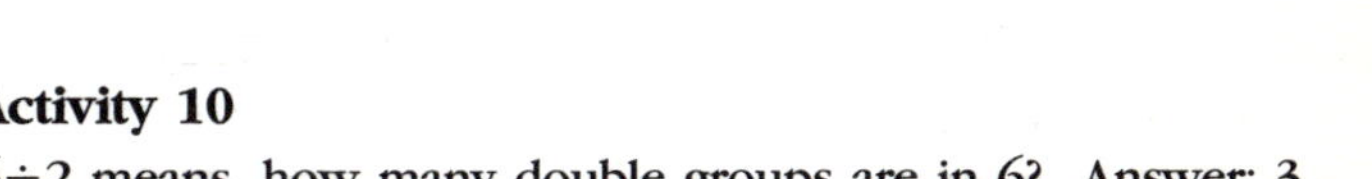

12 half-doughnuts in 6 doughnuts

Extending this to thirds, fourths, etc. leads your child to the next step, which is to find the reciprocal (invert or flip) of the divisor (second number) and multiply.

$$\text{First } 6 \div \frac{1}{2} = 6 \times \frac{2}{1}$$

$$= \frac{12}{1}$$

$$= 12$$

$$\text{Then try } \frac{5}{9} \div \frac{4}{7} = \frac{5}{9} \times \frac{7}{4}$$

$$= \frac{35}{36}$$

Now, have your chld write down this rule:

$$\frac{a}{b} \div \frac{c}{d} = \frac{a}{b} \times \frac{d}{c} \quad \text{and practice, practice, practice.}$$

The most common error when dividing fractions is to simply divide the denominator (*d*) into the numerator (*a*). Check to make sure your child is applying the rule properly.

DECIMALS

As a rule, children find decimals easier to work with than fractions. They grasp the place value concept (tenths, hundredths, thousandths, etc.) fairly easily, since so much of our life in Canada is based on the metric system and money, both of which use decimals extensively.

10	tens
1	units
0.1	tenths
0.01	hundredths
0.001	thousandths
0.0001	ten thousandths

But kids do encounter difficulties with arithmetic operations. Frequently, they will follow the techniques used with whole numbers, ignoring the special rules needed when working with decimals.

CONVERTING FRACTIONS TO DECIMALS (GRADE 4)

Activity 11

Although children generally convert fractions to decimals properly when taught in school, they frequently fall into the mistake of converting fractions to decimals in the following way: $\frac{5}{8} = 5.8$ or 0.58, instead of dividing the denominator into the numerator.

It comes down to helping your child understand that $\frac{5}{8}$ means 5 parts out of 8 parts. When converting to a decimal, it must be converted to tenths, hundredths, etc. That is precisely what division does.

$$\frac{5}{8} = 5 \div 8$$

$$= 0.625$$

$$\left(= \frac{6}{10} + \frac{2}{100} + \frac{5}{1000} \right)$$

(not 5.8 or 0.58)

If your child is prone to making this mistake, it may indicate a lack of understanding that a decimal is just a different form of writing fractions. It is imperative that he understand this concept before progressing to further work with decimals.

ADDING AND SUBTRACTING DECIMALS (GRADE 4-5)

Activity 12

The most frequent error made when adding or subtracting decimals is to improperly line up the decimal points. To overcome this, your child needs to review the meaning of each place value:

> All tenths must line up together, because they all have the same denominator (10). Similarly, all hundredths must line up together. Therefore, so must all the decimal points.

Give your child some squared (graph) paper. Have him write the first number, using one square for the decimal. All other numbers written below must have the decimal lined up with the first number's decimal. If your child has difficulties with the trailing blank spaces, when the numbers have different numbers of decimal places, he may fill them in with zeroes, providing he understands that it does not change the value of the number. Once the decimals are lined up, the rules are exactly the same as they are for whole numbers.

		2	.	5	1
		3	4	.	2
1	0	.	1	6	3
1	0.	5	6	1	6

Incorrect

	2	.	5	1	
3	4	.	2		
1	0	.	1	6	3
4	6	.	8	7	3

OR

	2	.	5	1	0
3	4	.	2	0	0
1	0	.	1	6	3
4	6	.	8	7	3

Correct with decimals lined up

MULTIPLYING DECIMALS (GRADE 5-6)

Activity 13

To help your child understand why we count the decimal places when multiplying, explore this by using a calculator and a pattern approach. Try this example:

$2800 \times 3.2 = 8960.0$	$600 \times 0.8 = 480.0$
$280 \times 3.2 = 986.0$	$60 \times 0.8 = 48.0$
$28 \times 3.2 = 98.6$	$6 \times 0.8 = 4.8$
$2.8 \times 3.2 = 9.86$	$0.6 \times 0.8 = 0.48$
$0.28 \times 3.2 = 0.986$	$0.06 \times 0.8 = 0.048$

Following this pattern, your child should see that the number of decimal places in the answer is the same as the total number of decimal places in the two original numbers. When using long multiplication, simply count the decimal places from the right-hand side of the number:

$$
\begin{array}{r l}
14.9 & \leftarrow 1 \text{ decimal place} \\
\underline{\times\, 2.1} & \leftarrow 1 \text{ decimal place} \\
149 & \\
\underline{2980} & \\
31.29 & \leftarrow 2 \text{ decimal places}
\end{array}
$$

Note: When multiplying, do not line up the decimals. Rather, line up the numbers along the right-hand side.

Follow this up with plenty of practice over a period of time, making sure your child writes down the number of decimal places, as shown above. Check to make sure the alignment of the columns is correct, because a common error when multiplying whole numbers or decimals is to misalign the partial products (149 and 2980, above).

DIVIDING DECIMALS (GRADE 5-6)

Just as with division of fractions, division of decimals can be described as finding the number of partial groups in a given number of groups. At this level, children will already know that \$0.25=25¢ and that 0.1 cm=1 mm. These can be used to help explain why the decimal is "moved over" when dividing.

Activity 14

Ask your child how many quarters (25¢) are in \$1.50. He will probably give the correct answer as 6. Ask him how he would use long division to answer the question and she should divide using whole numbers:

$$\begin{array}{r} 6 \\ 25\overline{)150} \\ \underline{150} \\ 0 \end{array}$$

Have him look at it in a different way, i.e., "How many \$0.25 coins are in \$1.50?" and he can see that moving the decimal to the right allows him to use whole numbers.

The next step comes with examples resulting in decimal answers, such as, "How many \$0.25 coins are in \$1.60?" When working with whole numbers, your child would have left a remainder. Now, decimal answers are required. A decimal must be placed after the 160, with zeroes inserted as necessary. Also, place a decimal immediately above in the answer (*quotient*). Then divide, just as with whole numbers, but keep going after the decimal, inserting and bringing down zeroes where necessary.

```
      6.4
25)160.0   ← Insert and bring down a zero.
   150
    100
    100
      0
```

There are 6.4 \$0.25 coins in \$1.60.

Once he understands that the decimal is moved to make it easier to divide (by using whole numbers), he will need to have a set of steps or rules as a reminder.

Have your child write down this set of steps in a prominent place in his notebook, keeping it as a reference until he consistently gets correct answers.

```
         quotient         6.4
divisor)dividend     25)160.0
                        150
                         100
                         100
                           0
```

- If the *divisor* contains a decimal, move the decimal to its far right.
- In the *dividend*, move the decimal the same number of spaces to the right.
- In the *quotient*, place a decimal immediately above the decimal in the *dividend*.
- Divide, just as with whole numbers, inserting zeroes in the *dividend* where necessary.

CHAPTER FIVE

Helping with percents
(Grades 6-7)

Children tend to experience a great deal of difficulty with percents. It is a relatively complex area of study for them. Percents are related to whole numbers, fractions and decimals, in addition to being used in problem solving. However, there are a few tips to help your child with the number relationships and with problem solving.

THE CONCEPT OF A PERCENT (GRADE 6-7)

Activity 1

The first concept your child must understand is that a percent is simply a different method of writing a fraction or a decimal.

15% is the same as $\frac{15}{100}$ which is the same as 0.15.

175% is the same as $\frac{175}{100}$ whtich is the same as 1.75.

2% is the same as $\frac{2}{100}$ which is the same as 0.02.

Have your child look for patterns in the box above. She should see that the fraction has a denominator of 100. To convert to a decimal, simply move the decimal point 2 places to the left. She should practice this with a few more examples before progressing to an activity where she starts with a fraction or decimal and converts to the other two forms:

Percent	Fraction	Decimal
5		
	$\frac{17}{100}$	
		4.81

Answers:

Percent	Fraction	Decimal
25	$\frac{25}{100}$	0.25
17	$\frac{17}{100}$	0.17
481	$\frac{481}{100}$	4.81

If your child still seems confused with these conversions, you may wish to go back to the section of chapter 4, Converting fractions to decimals (Activity 11).

WORKING WITH PERCENTS (GRADE 7)

"Do I multiply or divide?" When problem solving with percents, it is easy to get confused with the required methods. Knowing how to set up the solution and knowing which operations to use are the stumbling blocks. Most children will experience some difficulties in this area at some time.

Activity 2

Teach your child to use a **percent box**. In a percent box, all she needs to do is to fill in the known quantities and follow a consistent series of steps to solve the problem. The percent box is set up as shown:

part	*percent*
whole	*100*

Example: Find 30% of 80.

The percent is 30, the whole is 80. We need to find the part.

part	30
80	100

1. Set up a proportion equation: $\frac{part}{80} = \frac{30}{100}$

2. Cross multiply by the denominator (80) of the unkown (*part*):

$$part = 80 \times \frac{30}{100}$$

$$part = \frac{2400}{100}$$

$$part = 24$$

30% *of* 80 *is* 24.

Example: Three out of four marbles are red. What percent are red?

The part is 3 and the whole is 4. We need to find the percent.

3	*percent*
4	100

1. Set up a proportion equation: $\frac{3}{4} = \frac{percent}{100}$

2. Cross multiply by the denominator (100) of the unkown (*percent*):

$$percent = 100 \times \frac{3}{4}$$

$$percent = \frac{300}{4}$$

$$part = 75$$

75% *of the marbles are red.*

A **percent box** works for almost any percent problem at this level. It is simple and uses a consistent set of steps. Have your child try a few more examples, especially those containing more complex wording. Prices, sales tax and percentage marks are themes that work well. Eventually, give her some problems involving percents greater than 100. Note that problems involving an unknown **whole** are not taught at this level.

Activity 3

Have your child search the newspapers for real-life uses of percents. Make these uses into percent problems. Two examples are shown here:

Example: Chapters is having a 30% off sale. What would the discount and sale price be for a $40 book?

part	30
40	100

$$\frac{part}{40} = \frac{30}{100}$$

$$part = 40 \times \frac{30}{100}$$

$$part = 12$$

The discount is $12 and the sale price is $28.

Example: Last year, there were only 10 cm of snow in March, but this year, there were 25 cm of snow. What was the percentage increase?

First, calculate the increase: $25 - 10 = 15$ cm

Percentage increase and decrease use the ***original*** value as the ***whole*** and the ***difference*** as the ***part***.

15	*percent*
10	100

$$\frac{15}{10} = \frac{percent}{100}$$

$$percent = 100 \times \frac{15}{10}$$

$$percent = 150$$

There was a 150% increase in snowfall.

CHAPTER SIX

Helping with measurement

(Grades 2-7)

MEASURING LENGTH

Most difficulties children have with linear measurements have to do with context. They have little sense of what a mm, cm, m or km looks or feels like. You can help your child with linear measurement with easy activities around the home.

BEGINNING METRIC MEASUREMENT (GRADE 2-3)

Activity 1

Start by looking at a 30 cm ruler with him and showing him the cm and mm markings. Have him count the number of mm in a cm and the number of cm in a 30 cm ruler. Then get him to measure common objects around the home, such as a table, some toys, a book, etc. Measuring body parts is very useful, because at least one part of a child's hand will be 1 cm long (usually across 1 finger) and can serve as an easy reference. Progress to your child estimating distances before actually measuring the objects.

Be careful when using a ruler to begin measuring at the 0 mark, not necessarily at the edge of the ruler.

Activity 2

For measurements requiring a metre stick or measuring tape, again, first count the number of centimetres in one metre to show why we need a metre measurement. Measure longer distances, such as your child's room or a play area in the yard. Finish it off with a treasure hunt, written on a treasure map:

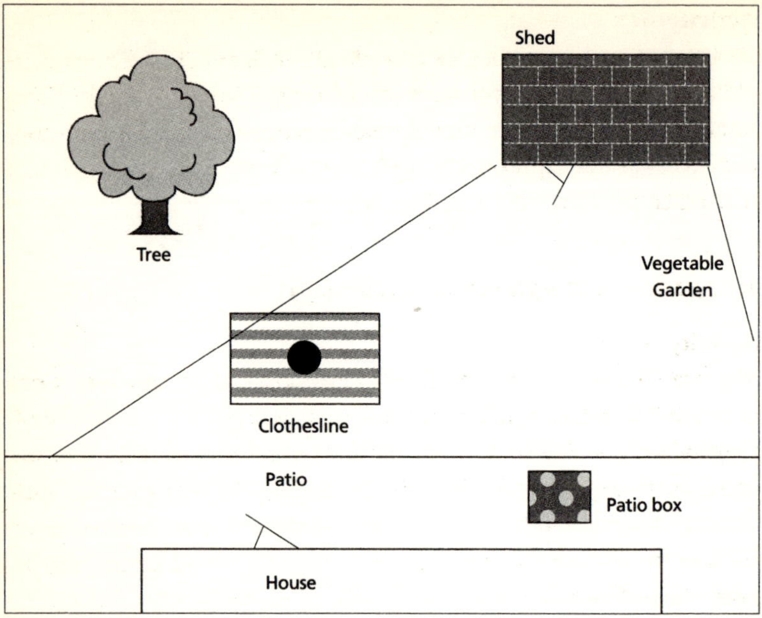

1. Start at the shed door.
2. Walk 5 m east toward the vegetable garden.
3. Walk southwest 2 m.
4. Walk south 4 m.
5. Walk 6 m toward the clothesline.
6. Walk south 3 m.
7. Walk 9 m toward the tree.
8. Walk 2 m east.

You should now be at the treasure.

Activity 3

You can also help your child build something, such as a birdhouse, using his new-found measurement skills. Start with your child planning the project on graph paper, checking to make sure the measurements will work out properly. Then, help him plan how much wood to purchase, estimate the cost of the materials and go to the local lumber store to buy them. Finally, he can measure, cut and build the project.

Activity 4

To help in understanding measurements in kilometres, show your child the odometer on your car when you are going to drive a short distance over 1 km. Have him announce when you reach 1 km, stopping to note the appropriate spot. Later, walk with your child to that place to show your child what a km "feels" like.

METRIC CONVERSIONS (GRADE 4-5)

Activity 5

In primary grades, converting between mm, cm, m and km is not necessary. In junior grades, children must first develop skills in multiplying and dividing by 10, 100 and 1000. Once the skills are in place and the concept is understood, you can help by showing the relationship between the units on a metre stick and that multiplying or dividing by 10, 100 or 1000 allows your child to select the appropriate unit of measurement for the particular object being measured. For example, show that 23 cm=230 mm. Following that, the best way to help with metric conversions is to design some worksheets similar to those provided by the teacher and let your child practice.

Metric Equivalents: 1000 mm = 1 m
100 cm = 1 m
10 mm = 1 cm
1000 m = 1 km

Other metric prefixes are not studied until high school.

An easy way of remembering the conversions is to build a scale:

mm	cm		m			km

To convert one step to the left, multiply by 10.
To convert two steps to the left, multiply by 100.
To convert three steps to the left, multiply by 1000.
To convert to the right, divide.

$$23 \text{ cm} \times 10 = 230 \text{ mm}$$

CIRCUMFERENCE OF A CIRCLE (GRADE 7)

Activity 6

Children frequently experience difficulties with circumference of a circle because of the new symbol, pi ($\pi=3.14$). To help your child understand the formula, $C=\pi d$, measure the distance a bicycle wheel turns in one rotation. Then measure the diameter of the wheel and multiply by 3.14 to get the circumference. You can show this with wheels or circles of various sizes and the answer will always be the circumference.

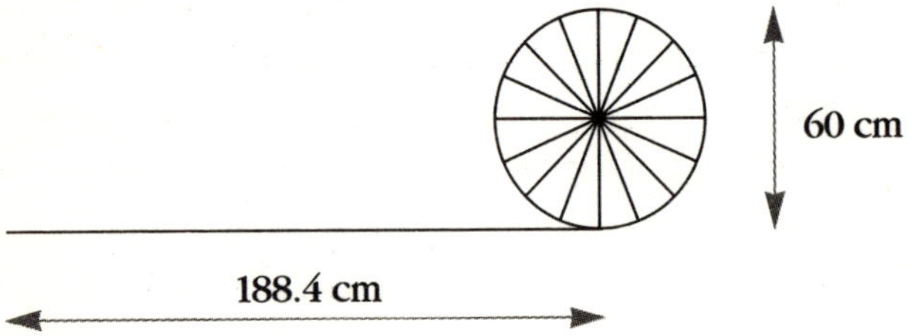

$$\begin{aligned} C &= \pi d \\ &= 3.14 \times 60 \\ &= 188.4 \text{ cm} \end{aligned}$$

For your child to remember the formula, use whatever memory techniques he normally uses for formulas. Practice exercises help too.

Activity 7

Your child can test the circumference formula using a tape measure around the house. Have him measure both the diameter and circumference of a large garbage can. Have him multiply the diameter by pi ($\pi=3.14$). The result should be fairly accurate.

For example, with a 50 cm diameter, the result should be $50\times3.14=157$ cm for the circumference.

Have him try measuring smaller objects. The results will be less accurate. Ask him why? The reason is that, as the objects we measure become smaller, the measurements require greater accuracy. Our tape measures and rulers are only accurate to the nearest mm.

MEASURING AREA

CONCEPT OF AREA (GRADE 2-3)

Activity 8

The concept of area is best taught using 1 cm^2 graph paper (easily purchased at your local office-supply store). Have your child draw a rectangular shape on a sheet of graph paper. Color and count all the squares covered. This is then the area of the rectangle in cm^2. Then have your child trace or draw an object, such as a leaf on the graph paper. Color and count the whole squares covered. Color the partial squares in a different color, estimating how many whole squares this would make. This can be done with a variety of more complex shapes as your child becomes more accurate in estimating.

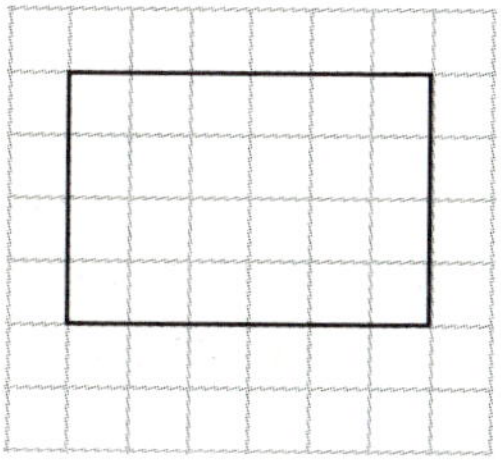

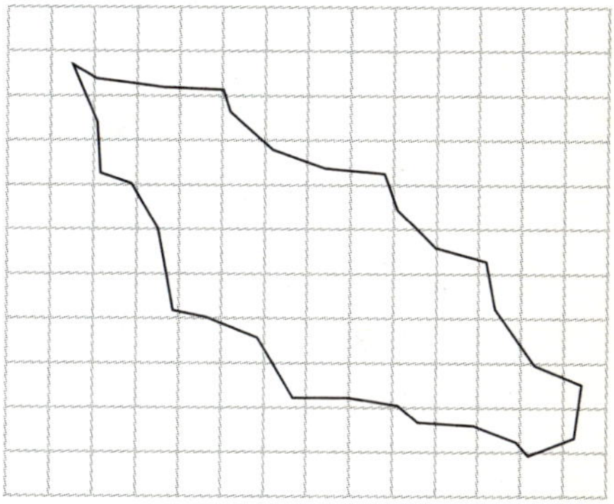

AREA OF A RECTANGLE (GRADE 4)

Activity 9

To teach the concept of **length** × **width**, place 12 candies in a 3 by 4 pattern on a sheet of graph paper. Have your child count the squares covered by candies. Repeat after rearranging the candies into a 2 by 6 pattern. Go back and have your child count the number of candies in the length and width. Ask her to think about the relationship between the dimensions and the area of a rectangle, that being **area = length × width**. The candies can be a reward for getting the answer correct.

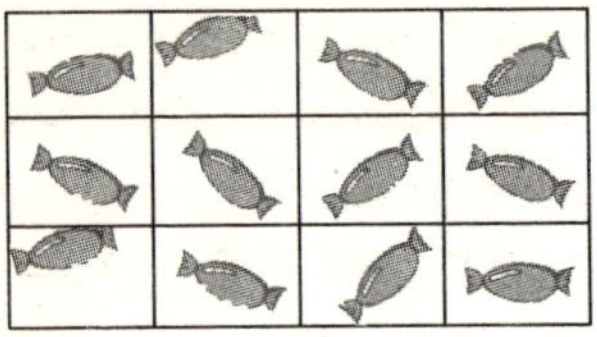

A 3 by 4 grid with 12 candies. This gives us $3 \times 4 = 12$.

Progress to measuring the areas of rectangular shapes around the home, including desktops, floor tiles, picture frames, etc. The candy activity can also be used to help your child with areas of triangles ($\frac{1}{2}$ **base × height**) and **parallelograms (base × height)**.

MEASURING VOLUME AND CAPACITY

CAPACITY OF CONTAINERS (GRADE 3-4)

Activity 10

Children need to understand capacity of containers before moving on to volumes of objects. Most measuring spoons and cups are labelled in metric (mL and L) in addition to imperial (tsp., cups). These are valuable tools in understanding capacity. Many children think the tallest or widest container has the greatest capacity. Give your child a variety of containers, in different sizes and shapes, allowing him to compare their capacities. He can then arrange them from least to greatest capacity. Discuss the differences in the dimensions of the containers (beyond the obvious tallest and widest) and how they affect the capacity. Follow that up with checking their approximate capacity in standard units. Remember to ask questions to encourage your child to compare, sort, estimate.

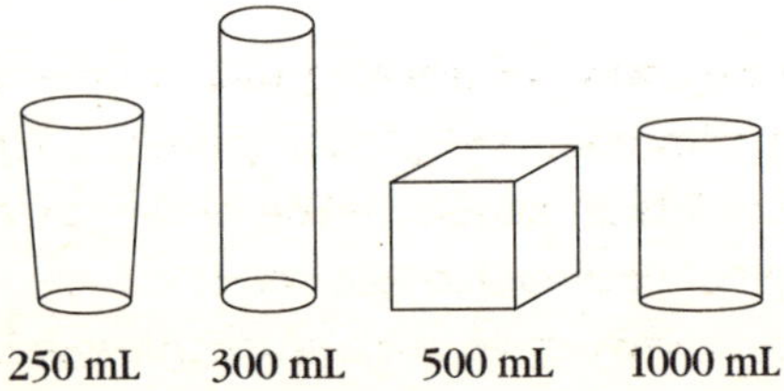

Activity 11
Children always enjoy making cookies. This can be a valuable learning activity too. Many cookbooks' recipes now include metric measurements. Choose a cookie recipe that requires accurate measurements in both mL and L. Let your child make the cookies with minimal help. This will give him greater confidence in his measurement abilities. This activity will also reinforce skills in measurement of area (cookie sheets), time and temperature.

VOLUMES OF SOLIDS (GRADE 6)

Activity 12
Volume of solid rectangular objects can easily be demonstrated with Lego-type blocks. Building rectangular solids help develop the formula **volume = length × width × height**, in the same manner as the area formula. Count the total number of blocks in the solid. Then count the number of blocks in each dimension and apply the formula, comparing with the counted total.

MONEY CONCEPTS

MONEY CONCEPTS (GRADE 3-5)

Activity 13
Because money comes in denominations of 2, 5, 10, 25, 50 and 100, children need to count by 2s, 5s, 10s, 25s, 50s and 100s. This helps them learn the relationships between the coins. A simple activity to assist them in this is to get out a number of coins of a single denomination and have your child count by 5s (for example). Progress to asking your child how he would make up 35¢, 80¢, $1.20, etc.

Activity 14
There are two easy ways of teaching money concepts to children: giving them an allowance and playing games. A regular allowance at an early age builds an understanding of the value of money and the relationship between dollars and cents. Let your child spend his allowance at the corner store, without supplementing it if he does

not have enough to buy a favorite candy or comic book. Because sales tax plays an important part of purchases, it helps to build an early foundation to understanding percents and decimals.

Activity 15
Many board games involve money. Monopoly, Stock Ticker and MoneyCents all teach money management skills, including understanding the values of different properties, growth of investments and making change.

MEASURING TIME

READING AND ESTIMATING TIME (GRADE 2-3)

Activity 16
Teaching your child to tell time can easily be done by having both an analog and a digital clock in the same room. Periodically compare them at significant moments of the day. Have your child read the time from the digital clock and describe the positions of the hands on the analog clock. Start with times on the hour, then $\frac{1}{2}$ hour, $\frac{1}{4}$ hour, $\frac{3}{4}$ hour, then by 5-minute intervals and finally by 1-minute intervals.

Activity 17
To help your child learn to measure or estimate elapsed time, use a digital watch or a stop watch. Measure the elapsed time to complete a task or to arrive at a chosen destination. Ask your child to estimate the elapsed time. He can then check it on the watch.

Activity 18
An excellent way of practicing telling time is with a homemade clock. Help your child construct a clock out of cardboard using a duotang pin to connect the hands to the face. Your child should print the numbers from 1 to 12 appropriately around the clock face. He can use the clock to practice telling time or as a reminder (silent alarm) clock.

CHAPTER SEVEN

Statistics: Venn diagrams, collecting data, graphs and averages

(Grades 2-7)

In school, children study statistics from kindergarten to graduation, though the word "statistics" is not generally used until about grade 4. It starts with measuring the children's heights or counting their missing teeth and plotting the results on a bar graph. It continues with classifying objects and shapes and illustrating the results with Venn diagrams. As your child gets older, the concepts become more complex. She'll begin working with line graphs, pictographs, circle graphs, fractions within the graphs, designing and conducting a survey and performing a detailed analysis of the data.

CLASSIFYING WITH VENN DIAGRAMS (GRADE 2-3)

At an early age, children begin classifying by color, size and quantity. These qualities are all known as "attributes." A Venn diagram is a rectangle containing circles, each representing a set of items, each with the same attributes. This type of diagram helps your child to visually and verbally classify items into two (possibly overlapping) groups.

Activity 1

Using two colored (e.g., red and green) rings, have your child classify a number of objects into "heavy" and "light." Have her follow that up by drawing the Venn diagram on a sheet of paper.

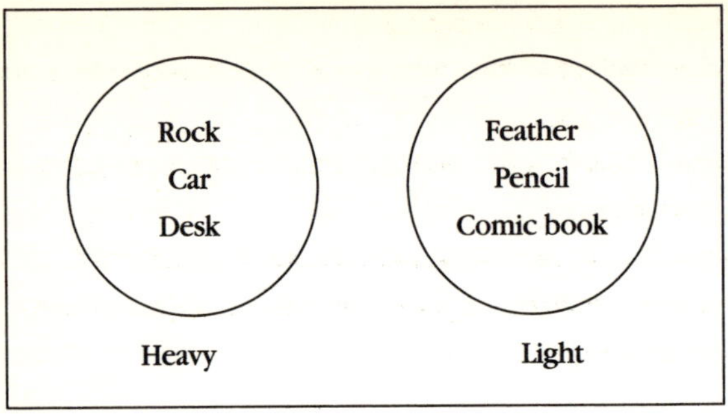

Continue this activity with two overlapping sets, such as story and picture books or lunch and dinner foods. The circles would intersect as shown below:

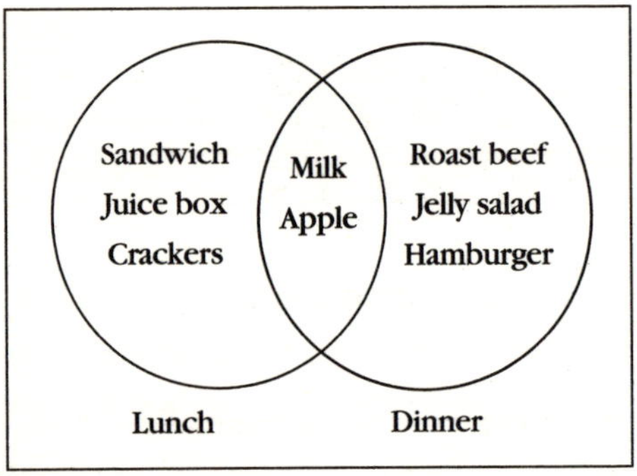

Finish this activity by drawing a Venn diagram containing items in which the attributes are not provided. Just the items are given. For example, you could use the lunch and dinner example, providing the circles with the foods included. Have your child try to come up with the lunch and dinner labels.

COLLECTING AND ORGANIZING DATA (GRADE 2-3)

Activity 2

Have your child make a **bar graph** of the most frequent colors found on her toys. Ask her to collect up to 20 toys made of a solid color and to separate them by color. She should then plot the results on a bar graph as follows:

- Use 1 cm square graph paper.
- Draw and label the horizontal axis to represent the names of the colors.
- Draw and label the vertical axis to represent how often each color occurs.
- Draw each bar, 1 square in width, with the number of squares vertically representing the number of toys of a specific color.

See the example below:

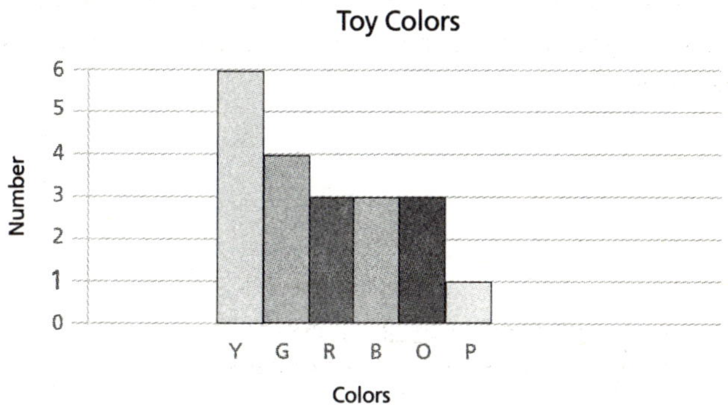

Your child could also plot this graph as a **pictograph**, in which each symbol represents a many-to-one correspondence. A picture of a toy could represent two toys of that color. Otherwise, it is plotted in the same manner as a bar graph. See Activity 3 for an example.

COLLECTING, ORGANIZING AND INTERPRETING DATA (GRADE 4-6)

Similar activities as in Activity 1 can be designed at this level. However, results should be tallied in a table or spreadsheet before graphing. As soon as your child has an understanding of fractions, pictographs can include the relationship that if 1 picture represents 10 people, then 0.5 pictures represents 5 people. Your child will be ready to interpret data generated from surveys and from preprinted graphs. Analysis of bias in reporting and in the survey questions should also be stressed.

Activity 3

Newspapers and magazines are a treasure trove of data. Find a graph containing data of interest to your child. To help her develop her data analysis skills, ask a few questions about the graph and encourage her to add to the list of questions. For example, the **pictograph** below represents the results of a survey on favorite sports:

Favorite Sports

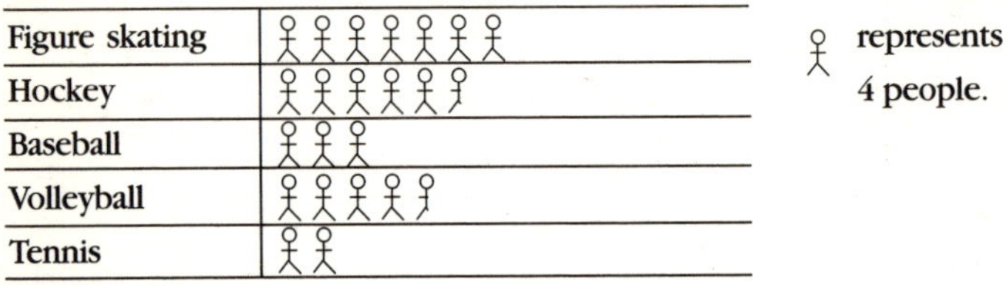

Possible questions you or your child could ask:

- How many votes did each sport receive?
- How many people took part in the survey?
- Which was the most popular sport?
- Which was the least popular sport?
- Which (if any) sports received the same number of votes?
- How many more people preferred figure skating over baseball?
- What other factors may have influenced the outcome of the survey? (grade 5)
- What could be done to limit the bias in the survey? (grade 6)

LINE AND CIRCLE GRAPHS (GRADE 6-7)

Line graphs are used to show measurements over a period of time. Time goes on the horizontal axis with the measurement on the vertical axis.

Activity 4

A fun activity is to plant a seed (preferably a bean or other fast-growing plant) and measure its height, every day at the same time, for two weeks. Plot the results on a line graph. This also makes a good science project.

Height of a Bean Plant at 6:00 p.m.

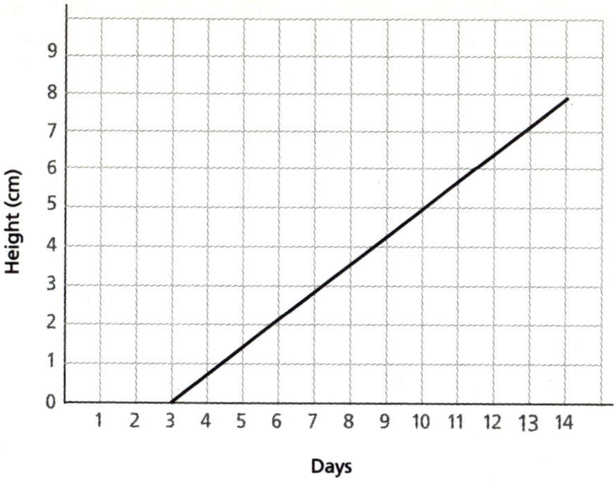

Circle graphs represent fractions or percentages of a total. To be able to properly use circle graphs, your child will need to be proficient at fractions and percents (see chapters 4 & 5 in this book).

Activity 5

Have your child categorize her CD or tape collection. She should then estimate, in eighths, the fraction each category is of her total CD collection. (Use eighths because it is easy to divide a circle into 8 parts.) She can then shade in the appropriate number of sections of a circle (divided into eighths) to represent each category.

Type of Music CDs

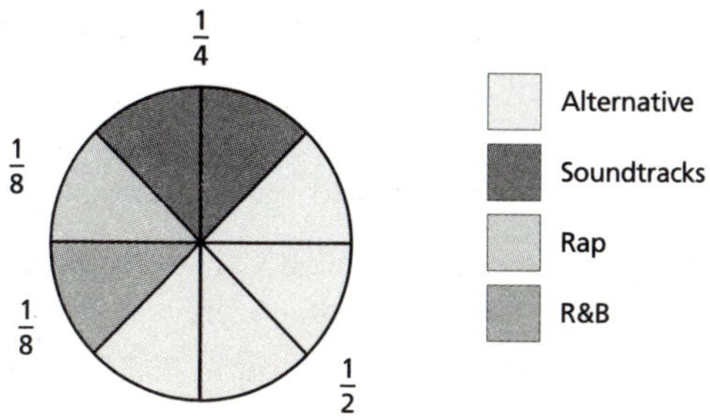

To draw this graph using percents, have your child calculate the percent (rounded to the nearest unit) for each category. Then multiply the percent by 360° and divide by 100 to calculate the angle of each section.

For example: If your child has 20 CDs and 6 of them are Rock,

$$\frac{6}{20} \times 100 = 30\%$$

$$30 \times 360 \div 100 = 108^\circ$$

Draw a radius in a circle. Place the protractor on the radius line and measure and mark 108°. Further sections can be made by placing the protractor on the new radius line.

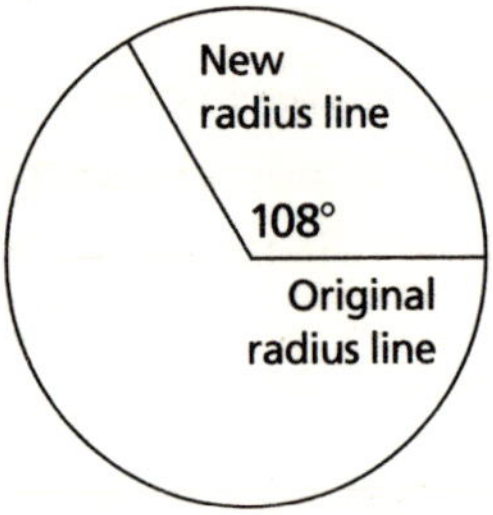

Labelling will then be done just as in the completed example above, except using percents instead of fractions.

MEASURING "AVERAGES": MEAN, MEDIAN, MODE (GRADE 7-8)

In earlier grades, children learn about averages, especially in the form of their average mark. In sports, statistics such as batting average and save percentage are well known. But how they are calculated causes confusion among even the most ardent sports fan. **Means** (or averages) are not the only measure of what mathematicians call "central tendency." **Median** (middle measurement when ranked from largest to smallest) and **mode** (most frequent measurement) are also important. Your child needs to practice and learn how to calculate each measure and understand which is most appropriate for a given set of data.

Activity 6

Have your child collect data for her favourite sport over a 1- or 2-week period. Here's a hockey example.

Goals scored by the players on your child's hockey team in a series of 5 games

Ryan	11	Tina	4	Sarah	4	Dan	4	Corey	3
Gail	2	Chang	2	Evan	1	Anna	1	Zena	1
Eddy	0	Ken	0	Tom	0	Khan	0	Deb	0

The **mean** would be (11+4+4+4+3+2+2+1+1+1+0+0+0+0+0)÷15=2.2 goals
The **median** would be the 8th (middle) of the 15 ranked measurements = 1 goal
The **mode** would be the most frequent = 0 goals (5 players scored 0 goals)

The **mean** is quite high due to the extreme value of 11 goals by Ryan.
The **mode** of 0 hardly represents the 10 players who scored at least 1 goal.
Therefore, the measure that best represents the "**average**" player on the team is the **median** = 1 goal.

This activity can be done with any sport or activity. It helps your child understand that the "average" occurrence is not necessarily the "mean."

Activity 7

Have your child search for both proper and improper use of mean, median and mode in newspapers and magazines. Teen and music magazines contain many statistics. Newspapers frequently include kids' pages containing data of interest to them. Of course, the sports section contains a vast array of data. Look for averages, rankings, ratings, most, least - any measure that denotes a comparison of data. Analyze the measures critically.

- Discuss whether the measure is an accurate representation of the person, team, company, group, etc.
- Discuss whether the calculations included all vital data.
- Are the data accurate measures or are they based on opinions?
- Ask "what if..." questions:

  "What if we divide by the number of people to make it per person?"

  "What if we take into consideration the weather?"

  "What if we throw out the extreme values?"

Statistics are often used to support a position being made by the author of the story. As such, they can easily be biased in their use. It is important that your child develop critical thinking skills when reading and interpreting data and summaries of data, such as graphs and averages. By high school, such understanding will be expected. Why not start early?

CHAPTER EIGHT

Helping with chance
(Grades 2-7)

UNDERSTANDING CHANCE (GRADE 2-5)

In early grades, children begin to develop an understanding of the concept of likelihood when solving simple problems. The progression is as follows:

- never/sometimes/always
- likely/unlikely/fair chance/probable/expected
- possible/impossible/certain/uncertain/equally likely/more likely/less likely
- more probable/less probable/equally probable/improbable/best/worst

The activities below are designed to get your child to the next level in understanding these relationships.

Activity 1

Play a game of **Guess a Color**. Place 4 red and 4 blue balls or marbles in a bag. Both you and your child predict the color of the ball that will be selected from the bag. Both players can make the same prediction. Select a ball and give 1 point for a correct guess. Return the ball to the bag. Repeat this for 10 tries. The winner is the player with the most points after the 10 tries.

To help your child understand chance, ask him the following questions:

- Is it more likely to pick a red or blue ball?
- Is it possible to pick a green ball?
- After a blue ball is selected, is it more likely that a red ball will be picked?

Alter the game by (a) using 8 red and 8 blue balls
(b) using 8 red and 4 blue balls
(c) not returning the balls after being picked

Ask the same questions as above to help understand how, in (a), the chances have not changed; in (b), the red balls are more likely; and in (c), the likeliness of each color is changed with each ball picked.

CALCULATING PROBABILITIES (GRADE 5-6)

Once children have a basic understanding of fractions, they are ready to apply it to calculating probabilities. They have little difficulty grasping the definition of probability:

$$\frac{\text{Number of successful outcomes}}{\text{Total number of outcomes}}$$

Be careful not to confuse probability with **odds**. Odds are a **ratio of opposite probabilities**. For example, the probability, when tossing a coin, of showing heads is $\frac{1}{2}$ as is the probability of showing tails. The odds, however, are $\frac{1}{2}:\frac{1}{2}$, or 1:1. Odds are not studied until high school and will not be discussed in this book.

Kids frequently need help in calculating and understanding probabilities based on an experiment. The activities below will help.

Activity 2

To show that, in an experiment, the results are frequently different from what is predicted, have your child toss a coin 50 times, recording the results each time. Using a tally method is probably best. Most likely, there will be a fairly uneven split in the results. This is because 50 tosses is a relatively small sample and runs of 8 or 10 heads or tails in a row are not uncommon.

Activity 3

Have your child determine the probabilities of each sum on a pair of dice by performing the following activity:

- Roll a pair of dice 100 times, recording the sum each time.
- Summarize in table form.
- Draw a bar graph of the results.
- Calculate the probability of each sum as

$$\frac{\text{number of occurrences}}{100}.$$

The following questions should be asked:

- Which is the most likely sum of the two dice?
- Which is the least likely sum?
- Which sums are equally likely?
- Compare the graph with your results. Is there a similarity?
- If you were to repeat this experiment, would the results be the same? Why?
- What would happen if you rolled the dice 200 times?

Hints to parents

The most likely sum is 7, the least likely are 2 and 12.
The results, when repeated, would be different because of probability.
Rolling the dice 200 times would give a more accurate set of results.

CALCULATING THEORETICAL PROBABILITIES (GRADE 6-7)

There is a big jump from calculating probabilities based on experiments to those based on theoretical results. Knowing there are 6 faces on a standard die, a child can easily understand that the probability of rolling a 5 is $\frac{1}{6}$. This is known as theoretical probability. To help your child understand more complex situations, have him complete the following activity.

Activity 4

In this activity, your child will calculate the theoretical probabilities for the sums when rolling two dice. Have your child complete Activity 8 (the graphing part is not necessary) and convert each probability to a decimal value. Then have him calculate the theoretical probabilities in the following way:

1. Set up a table of values with 1 to 6 across the top and 1 to 6 down the side.
2. Fill in the sums as shown below:

	1	2	3	4	5	6
1	1+1=2	1+2=3				
2	2+1=3					
3				3+4=7		
4						
5			5+3=8			
6						

3. Count the total number of outcomes (squares).
4. Count the number of squares containing each sum.
5. Calculate the probability of each sum as

$$\frac{\text{number of squares containing each sum}}{\text{total number of squares}}.$$

6. Convert each probability to a decimal value.
7. Compare the results with those from Activity 3.

There are 6×6=36 squares.

Example:

The sum of 4 exists in 3 squares.

Probability (of a sum of 4) $= \frac{3}{36}$

$=0.833$

Hint: The results will probably be different from activity 3, since they are based on an experiment, not calculations.

Types of questions to ask:

- Which sum is most likely? least likely?
- Which sums are equally likely?
- Are the results the same as in Activity 8? Why?
- What would help the results from Activity 8 become more accurate?
- Do the results on one roll affect the probability of a particular sum on the next roll?

This type of activity helps your child understand that theoretical probabilities are based on calculations. He'll also see that, in practice, the results mirror, but do not necessarily match, the calculated probabilities. This is because chance is involved in the experiment.

CHAPTER NINE

Helping with geometry

(Grades 3-7)

WORKING WITH TWO-DIMENSIONAL SHAPES (GRADE 3-5)

Identifying geometric shapes can become a vocabulary nightmare. In primary grades, kids easily learn to identify basic shapes such as circles, squares, triangles and octagons. As your child progresses, it comes down to understanding the differences between **squares**, **rectangles**, **triangles**, **parallelograms**, **rhombuses** and **trapezoids**. Once your child knows her vocabulary, she can work with the shapes in a variety of ways. By the end of grade 5, she should be able to describe, in detailed language, the properties of these shapes, how to draw them, and how they are related to each other.

Square
four equal sides
all angles 90°

Rectangle
opposite sides equal
all angles 90°

Triangle
three-sided polygon

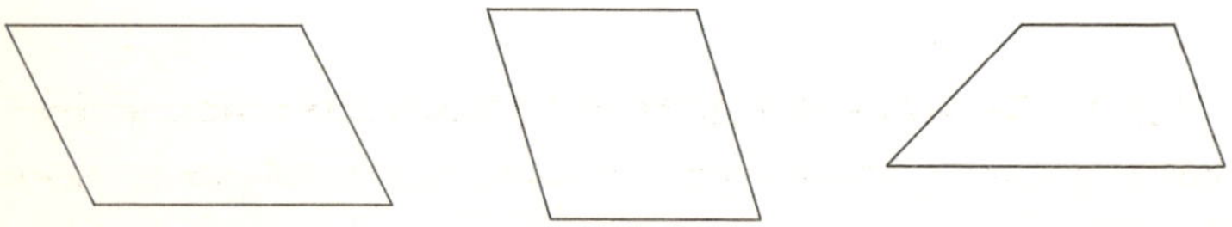

Parallelogram
opposite sides parallel
opposite sides equal

Rhombus
opposite sides parallel
all four sides equal

Trapezoid
one pair of
parallel sides

Activity 1

The diagram below is called a tangram. Your child should be familiar with it from school. It can be drawn on a piece of Bristol board or construction paper and cut along the lines. Have your child use the shapes available to create other squares, triangles, parallelograms, etc. Each time she constructs a new shape, she should identify it to you. She should also record how many of each shape she has constructed.

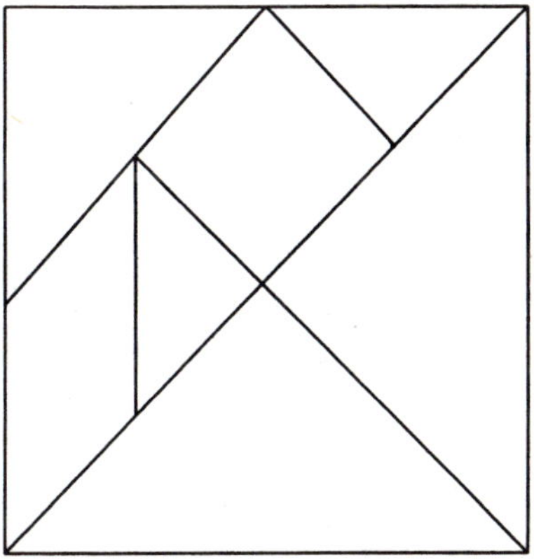

Activity 2

To practice her vocabulary and ability to use mathematical language, have your child draw a geometric shape, cover it up and describe it to you. She should describe it in as much detail as possible using mathematical vocabulary, but not the name of the geometric shape (e.g., triangle or parallelogram). As she is describing it, you draw the shape on a piece of paper. If she described it properly, your diagram should match hers.

UNDERSTANDING CUBES AND OTHER SOLIDS (GRADE 2-3)

Children generally know their two-dimensional shapes by grade 2. They frequently have difficulties making the jump to three-dimensional objects and the vocabulary associated with them.

Activity 3

Spend some time with your child, searching for examples of **cubes**, **cones**, **cylinders**, **spheres**, **pyramids**, **triangular prisms** and **rectangular prisms** in real life. Each time your child sees one of these objects, she should call it by its correct name. If you are able to accumulate some of these objects, ask the following questions:

- Which objects stack easily? Why?
- Which objects have circular faces?
- Which objects have rectangular faces?
- Which objects have triangular faces?
- Which objects have flat sides?
- Which objects have pointed tops?

At this point, do not have her draw the objects in two-dimensions. This is a skill that is developed in grades 5 and 6.

Activity 4

Ask your child to close her eyes (or blindfold her). Give her one of the solids mentioned in Activity 1. Ask her to describe the solid, based on the number and shapes of faces (surfaces), corners, edges and other properties. Ask if it would roll or slide when pushed. This activity develops your child's ability to visualize three-dimensional solids.

BUILDING SOLIDS FROM NETS (GRADE 3-5)

Children enjoy building solids from nets. However, they often get confused with the appropriate shapes, and their placement, in the net. (A net is a "flattened," two-dimensional drawing which, when cut out, can be folded to give a solid object.)

Activity 5

Have your child investigate nets by cutting open cardboard boxes. Rectangular prisms are readily available. Toblerone bars come wrapped in a triangular prism, for instance. Challenge your child to build her own and to extend her skills to pyramids, cones and cylinders. They can be decorated and put on display in her bedroom.

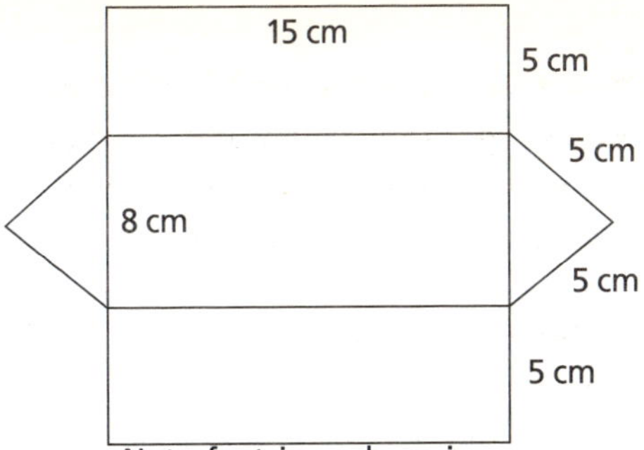

Net of a triangular prism

SKETCHING THREE-DIMENSIONAL SOLIDS (GRADE 4-6)

As a child gets older, her mathematical maturity enables her to think more abstractly. Drawing three-dimensional objects is one such abstraction.

Activity 6

Gather a few magazines or newspapers. Search through them with your child to find drawings of three-dimensional objects (cones, prism, cylinders, pyramids, spheres). Then have her use a draw program on a computer to sketch the 3D solids. If you do not have a computer, she can draw them by hand. She can follow this up by creating a design made entirely from sketches of 3D solids.

MEASURING ANGLES WITH PROTRACTORS (GRADE 6-7)

Activity 7

Record the movement of the stars. It is fairly easy to make a string protractor that your child can use to measure the angles of elevation of the stars. The small protractors available in math sets are okay, but if you can find a larger one at a school-supply store (probably only 25¢), it would work better. Tape a 60 cm piece of string to the center of the protractor. Hold the protractor against your cheek so that the base is level and the taped end of the string is placed directly at the position of the eye. Look at the star or object in question and extend the string toward it. Have a second person read the angle of elevation on the protractor. You can repeat this process every half hour to record the movement of the stars. You can adapt this activity to measure a wide variety of angles related to distant objects.

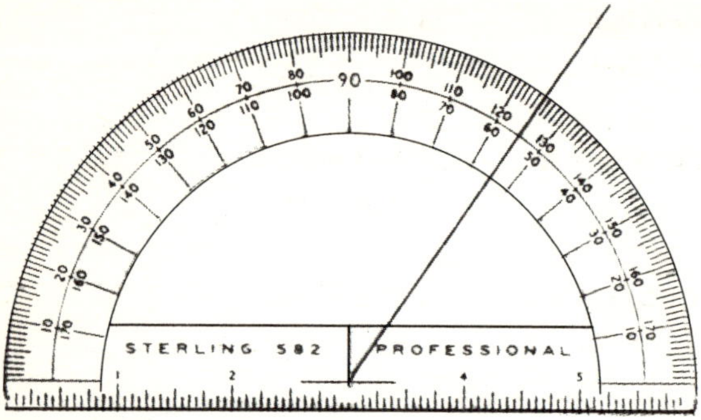

ANGLES AND PARALLEL LINES (GRADE 7-8)

Frequently children do not understand the angle properties of parallel lines. In many cases this is because they may not have not investigated the properties by measuring the angles.

Activity 8

To help your child understand these properties or traits, have your child use tangrams (see Activity 1) to create parallel lines. Any line joining two parallel lines is called a **transversal**. Have your child measure and record each angle with a protractor. This should be repeated with different sets of parallel lines and transversals. Ask her to investigate the similarities between the two diagrams and to identify the angle properties of parallel lines and a transversal that are not true for non-parallel lines.

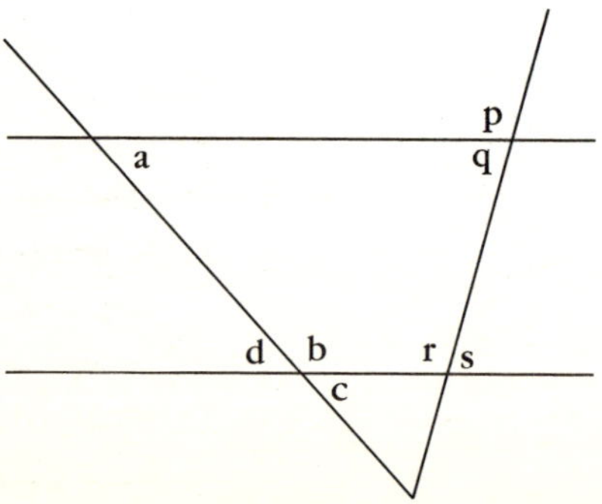

There are three properties, or traits. (The first two should be obvious. She may need help with the third.)

Trait	Example		
1. Corresponding angles are equal	a = c = 40° p = r = 110°	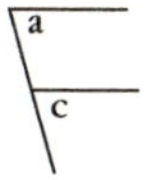	F-pattern
2. Alternate angles are equal	a = d = 40° q = s = 70°	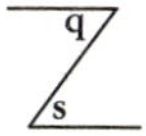	Z-pattern
3. Interior angles add to 180°	a + b = 180° q + r = 180°	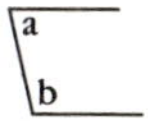	C-pattern

Once she has developed these properties, most difficulties come from not recognizing these and other properties of angles. Again, using a protractor to investigate further properties helps your child understand and recognize them.

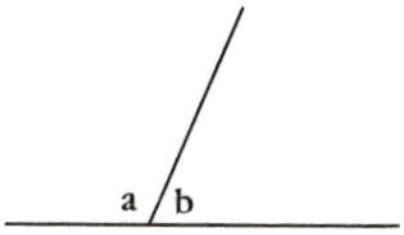

Supplementary angles add to 180°: a+b=180°

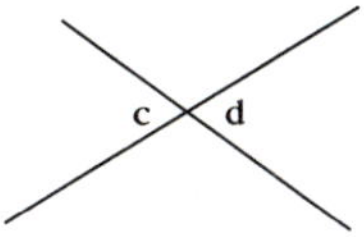

Vertically opposite angles are equal: c=d

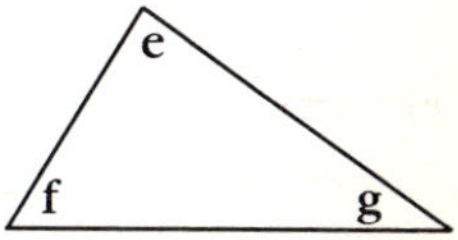

Sum of the angles of a triangle is 180°: e+f+g=180°

At this point, your child should be able to tackle the homework exercises in her textbook in which some angles are provided. The other angles need to be determined without a protractor, using the properties listed above.

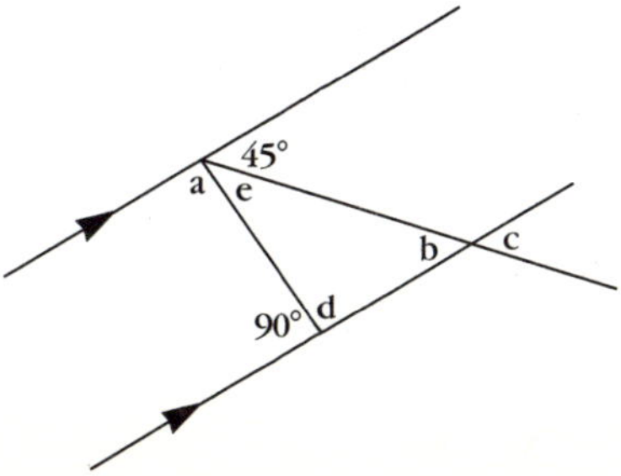

Answers:
a=90° (interior angles)
b=45° (alternate angles)
c=45° (corresponding angles or opposite angles)
d=90° (supplementary angles)
e=45° (sum of the angles of a triangle)

CHAPTER TEN

Graphing and transformations

(Grades 2-7)

Graphing is an important mathematical skill that becomes highly developed in high school. In elementary school, children first learn to read a compass and a map. They then progress to plotting points, first as whole numbers, then as integers and fractions.

UNDERSTANDING A COORDINATE GRID (GRADE 2-3)

Activity 1

Map reading is an important skill for many subjects at school. The geography and language components are obvious. Mathematics enters the picture with your child reading and understanding the coordinate locations on a map. Whenever you are going on a family trip, give your child the job of navigator. Have him locate your destination, its coordinates (e.g., F7) and its direction on a compass (e.g., SW). Have him locate other towns along the way in the same manner.

USING A COORDINATE GRID (GRADE 4-6)

Activity 2

The game of Battleship is an easy game to learn and is an excellent introduction to understanding locations on a grid. Most children already know the rules and play the game using a hand-drawn grid or a sheet of graph paper. You can also purchase the game produced by Milton Bradley.

Activity 3

To help your child practice plotting points from ordered pairs on a graph, draw a simple picture on a grid, using straight lines only. Label each point with an ordered pair as shown below (use positive values only - avoid negatives).

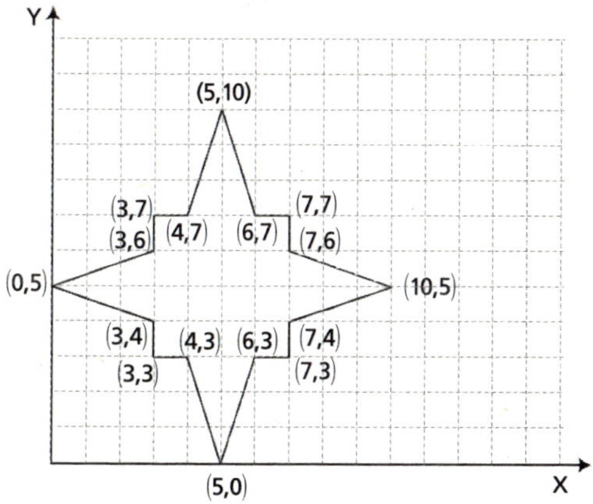

Then give your child the ordered pairs to be plotted in order and then joined to match your picture:

(5,0)→(4,3)→(3,3)→(3,4)→(0,5)→(3,6)→(3,7)→(4,7)→(5,10)→(6,7)→(7,7)→(7,6)→(10,5)→(7,4)→(7,3)→(6,3)→(5,0)

If he follows this order, he will reproduce your diagram. This is really like a kids' connect-the-dots puzzle. By about grade 6, your child should be able to make his own picture for you to reproduce.

Children frequently get confused with the plotting order of the coordinates of the ordered pair. Make sure your child plots points in the (x,y) order: **x units horizontal** followed by **y units vertical**. As well, check that he plots points **on the lines**, **not in the spaces**. The spaces between the lines represent fractions. (This type of confusion arises because **bar graphs** are plotted between the lines.)

UNDERSTANDING SYMMETRY (GRADE 2-3)

Symmetry is introduced to children by looking at the world around them. Children investigate symmetry in letters (e.g., A, B, M) and numbers (e.g., 3, 8, 11), playing cards and flags.

Activity 4

Children enjoy making paper crafts. Paper-folding activities help to demonstrate symmetry. Good examples include paper snowflakes, paper dolls and paper airplanes. Children also enjoy making pop-up greeting cards where folded paper pops up when the card is opened. Appreciating and understanding symmetry through art provides a foundation to further learning about transformations in mathematics.

SLIDES (TRANSLATIONS) ON A GRID (GRADE 4-5)

Children need to learn how simple movement does not affect the size and shape of an object. They also need to develop the communication skills to describe that movement.

Activity 5

Using a sheet of graph paper, have your child draw a map from home to his school or the local park. Each square might represent 1, 5 or 10 steps, whichever is most appropriate. He should then describe, in words, his path from home to his destination. (This will also help to develop his measurement, estimation and graphing skills)

Activity 6

Using a sheet of graph paper, draw a simple shape. Have your child draw its image after a slide or movement of, say, 5 steps up and 6 steps right. Repeat this with a more complex diagram. Geometric shapes and letters of the alphabet are ideal shapes to use since they are recognizable shapes. A properly drawn diagram should indicate to him that only the position will change, not the size or orientation of the parts.

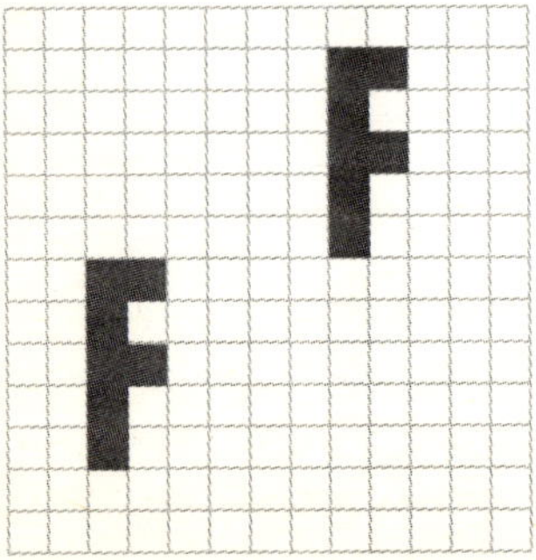

5 steps up and 6 steps right

FLIPS (REFLECTIONS) AND TURNS (ROTATIONS) (GRADE 6-7)

In grades 6 and 7, the study of transformations progresses to reflections and rotations, as well as combining two or more transformations. Many of the excellent tools used in schools (such as a Mira - a semi-transparent sheet of plexiglass that aids in drawing reflections) are not readily available to the public. The following activities can easily be done using regular student math equipment.

Activity 7

A pentimino is a set of 5 squares that can be manipulated to form various shapes. The following is an example of a pentimino shifted into 3 different shapes. This is an easy method of describing translations.

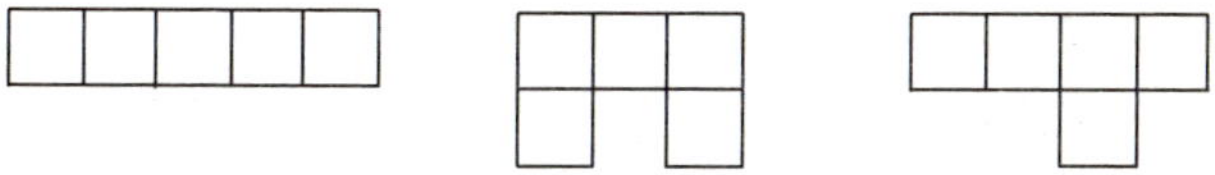

Make 2 pentiminos out of cardboard. To help with reflections, make a shape from one of them. Draw a horizontal or vertical line and ask your child to draw the reflected image, with the line acting as the mirror. All points in the image should be the same distance from the mirror as with the original shape, except flipped.

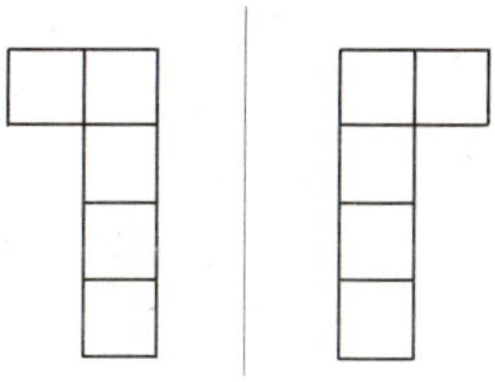

This is now a chance for your child to engage in problem creating:

- What if the mirror were diagonal?
- What if I changed the shape of the pentimino?

  … and so on.

To help with rotations, use a protractor to draw a 90° angle. Make a pentimino shape on one arm of the angle. Have your child draw a rotated image on the other arm of the angle. The image should have turned as shown below, but still otherwise unchanged.

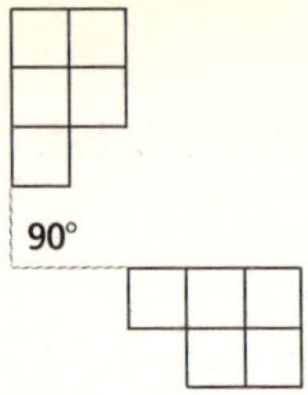

Again, this is a chance for your child to engage in problem creating:

- What if the angle were 180°?
- What if the angle were 60°?

  … and so on.

TILINGS (TESSELLATIONS) (GRADE 6-7)

Most people know tessellations as tilings, quilt patterns, wall paper patterns or M.C. Escher art. Simple tilings involve only slides and can be designed using the technique described in Activity 8. More complex tilings involve combinations of flips, slides and turns.

Activity 8

Teach your child to create his own simple tiling art in the following way:

(a) Draw a square.
(b) Cut a shape from one side.
(c) Move it to the other side of the square and tape together.
(d) Cut another shape from the top.
(e) Move it to the bottom of the square and tape together.
(f) You now have a basic shape that can be used as a template.
(g) Draw and cut out the shape in two or more colors.
(h) Fit the colored shapes together to create a tiling.

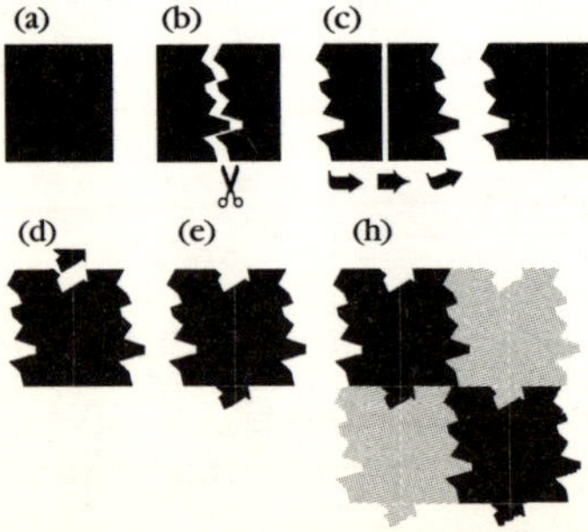

CHAPTER ELEVEN

Helping with introductory algebra

(Grades 5-7)

Algebra is the first highly abstract area of mathematics that children study. Understandably, it is the area where many students first encounter difficulties in math. The key is to approach algebra as a symbolic language. This language has very few rules when compared to spoken languages such as English or French.

PATTERNS (GRADE 5-7)

Activity 1

If your child is having difficulties with algebra, start by investigating and extending some simple counting patterns. Some examples are shown below. (Answers in brackets)

1, 3, 5, 7, 9, _____, _____ [11, 13]

2, 4, 8, 16, 32, _____, _____ [64, 128]

97, 92, 87, 82, 77, _____, _____ [72, 67]

1, 2, 2, 3, 3, 3, _____, _____, _____, _____ [4, 4, 4, 4]

1, 1, 2, 3, 5, 8, 13, _____, _____ [21, 34]

The next stage in algebra is to learn to build patterns in a table of values. Your child should then summarize in words, then as a mathematical expression and then extend the pattern for larger quantities. This is described in the following examples.

Activity 2

Use toothpicks to develop the following pattern and to describe the number of squares in a given diagram. (Answers are in brackets.)

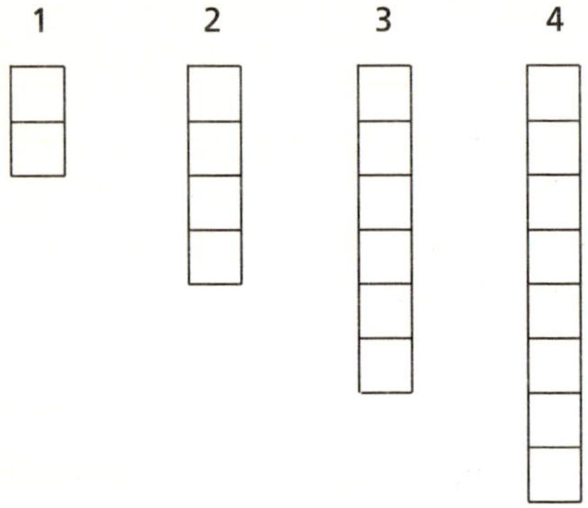

(a) Build a table of values showing the number of squares in each diagram.

Diagram #	# of Squares
1	2
2	4
3	6
4	8

(b) Describe the pattern. (The number of squares is double the diagram number.)

(c) Write an expression for the number of squares in diagram x. ($2x$)

(d) How many squares would be in diagram #20? ($2 \times 20 = 40$ There would be 40 squares in diagram #20.)

Activity 3

Your child probably knows what a three-legged race is – two people together with 2 legs tied to end up with 3 legs instead of 4. What if we tie 3 people's legs? Or 4 people's? Or x people's?

# of People	# of "Legs"
2	3
3	4
4	5
5	6
x	$x+1$

Because there is always 1 more "leg" than people, we can say that there are $x+1$ "legs" for x people.

Activity 4

You can make counting patterns that result in simple expressions. Some simple ideas to use:

- Children holding hands. How many hand-holds are there? (See graphical solution below.)
- Join some blocks together. How many faces are showing? How many edges?
- Shelving units side-by-side. How many shelves? How many pieces of wood?

This is a great opportunity to get your child to think and experiment with "what if..." questions: What if I count the number of toothpicks? What is the relationship between the number of shelves and the number of pieces of wood? Asking these questions and searching for a relationship will help to expand her mathematical imagination. Problem creating is an important adjunct to problem solving.

GRAPHS OF RELATIONS (GRADE 6-7)

The graphical representation of patterns is handled in two ways: by plotting the results of an activity and by analyzing a given graph.

Activity 5

This example plots a graph of the toothpick investigation in Activity 1. Have your child rewrite the table as a list of ordered pairs:

(1, 2), (2, 4), (3, 6), (4, 8) which, in turn, become points on a graph. On a sheet of graph paper, have her:

- draw the **x-axis** and **y-axis**
- plot and label each point
- label the graph fully as shown

Children often have difficulty deciding which quantity belongs on the horizontal and vertical axes. Remember, the quantity she starts with (i.e., the label or item number) belongs on the horizontal axis. The resulting measurement or calculation belongs on the vertical axis.

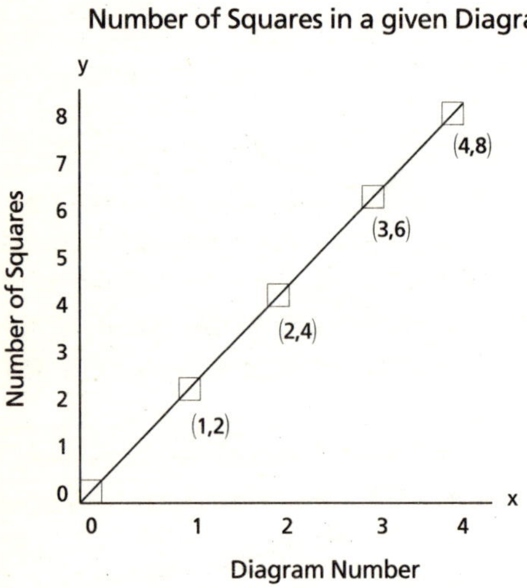

Ask your child to look at the resulting graph and to describe it in as many ways as possible. As long as the responses are correct, none is improper.

Activity 6

Children need to be able to analyze a relationship from a given graph. Give her a graph such as the following one.

Number of Hand-holds when Children Hold Hands in a Line

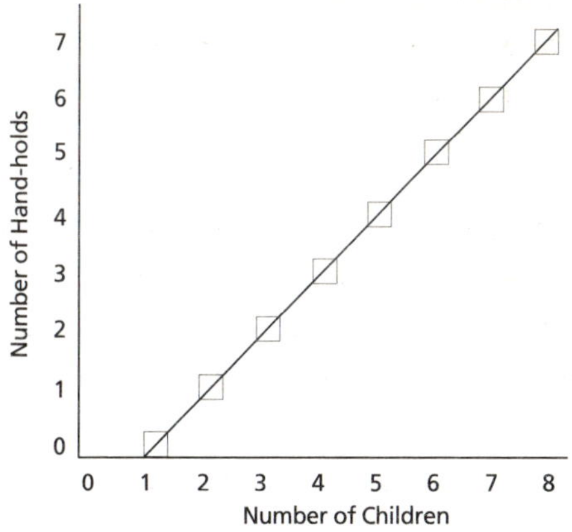

Ask the following questions (the answers are in brackets):

(a) How many hand-holds are there for 2 children? (1)

(b) How many hand-holds are there for 3 children? (2)

(c) How many hand-holds are there for 7 children? (6)

(d) Write a rule, in words, for the number of hand-holds if you know the number of children.
(There is one fewer hand-hold than the number of children.)

(e) How many hand-holds, H, are there for C children?
$(H = C - 1)$

When designing graphical examples, make sure they are straight lines. Curves have much more complex equations, not studied until high school.

THE CONCEPT OF A VARIABLE (GRADE 6-7)

Students frequently ask their teachers, "But what is x?" when looking at an expression such as $3x+2$. This generally means that they do not understand the concept of a variable or unknown.

Activity 7

Go back to the Patterns activities (#1, 2, 3, 4) above and discuss how x represents the diagram number, number of children, number of blocks or number of shelving units. The formula allows your child to use mathematical symbols in an expression to define the number of squares, hand-holds, etc.

Activity 8

Alternatively, ask your child to write down the formula for the area of a rectangle: $A = L \times W$. Then ask her, "What is *L*?" Her response will probably be, "The length." At this point, ask her, "What is the length?" and let it lead to a discussion of *L*, *W* and *A* being storage places for sets of values, all of which can make the equation or formula true. Similarly, a variable, x, represents a set of numbers, all of which would make the expression $3x+2$ correct. Illustrate how substituting different values for x results in different values for the expression.

Therefore, if $x=1$, $3x+2=3(1)+2$
$=3+2$
$=5$

Reminder:
$3x+2$ means
$3\times$(the value of x) plus 2.

if $x=2$, $3x+2=3(2)+2$
$=6+2$
$=8$

if $x=3$, $3x+2=3(3)+2$
$=9+2$
$=11$

. . . and so on.

Have your child continue the substituting as above. Then she can investigate the resulting pattern in the answers. You may be surprised, though, at the different patterns your child may see. Children see patterns differently from adults, often from a different perspective. If the patterns are correct, let her know, even if it is different from the one you are looking for. (In the example above, one child might see the pattern as tripling the x value and adding 3. Another child might see that you add 3 to get successive terms.)

Math teachers like to use x as a preferred variable or unknown. There is no rule, however, against using any letter of the alphabet. If your child wishes to use a favorite letter, by all means let her.

SOLVING SIMPLE EQUATIONS (GRADE 7)

Children first learn to solve equations by substituting and simplifying. This is commonly known as the "guess and check" method. Your child's textbook should have numerous exercises of this type. If you prefer to make them up by yourself, ensure that the answers are only whole numbers, not fractions, decimals or integers at this point.

Activity 9

To solve $3x+5=29$, she would "guess" a value for x, substitute and simplify to check if the result is 29. The "guessing" is more of an educated guess, based on estimation skills.

Guess	Check
If $x=7$:	$3\times7+5=27$ (too small)
If $x=9$:	$3\times9+5=32$ (too big)
If $x=8$:	$3\times8+5=29$ (correct)

Most children come up with the answer of $x=8$, some very quickly, some fairly slowly. Each time your child guesses incorrectly, she should think about two things before revising her guess: How close am I? Is the number too big or too small? Eventually, she will zero in on the correct answer.

Students are not taught a formal method of solving equations until grade 8 or 9, depending on the jurisdiction. This will not be covered in this book.

CHAPTER TWELVE

Some tips on...

MATHEMATICS SOFTWARE

Computer software can be a valuable tool in motivating your child to do mathematics and in providing practice in a variety of skills. Mathematics software can come in many different formats: arcade games, adventures, simulations, exploration and drill. Good software provides your child with encouragement and incentives to continue. Otherwise, he will simply turn the computer off. The following are some important questions you need to consider:

- ***Does the software address a variety of skills?***
  It is important that the software teach many different skills. Children will only practice a particular skill for a short period of time before moving on.
- ***How is a math drill presented to the child?***
  Drill is a very important component of any software. Equally important is how it is presented. If it is presented simply as drill, the child is turned off immediately. If it is presented as a competition (arcade, race, etc.) against the computer or the clock, this adds interest and excitement. Drill should also be enhanced with graphics. Animals, money, toys and other items normally of interest to the child help to disguise drill and hold attention longer.

- ***What is the theme of the software?***
  Software with a theme of interest to the child is a good motivator. Solving a mystery, climbing a mountain, driving a race car, running a town and operating an amusement park are just a few successful themes. The theme can be story-based or it can simply be a connector between various activities.

- ***Is there enough variety to keep the child's interest?***
  As the saying goes, "Variety is the spice of life." This is true with math software, as well. As was mentioned above, a variety of skills should be addressed. Reading and problem-solving skills should be integrated into the activities. Make sure there is a mixture of activities and types of activities. For example, if a child is successful in an arcade game, he is "rewarded" by being presented with a problem-solving activity. If your child has reading difficulties, let him try reading the problems out loud to you first. If necessary let an adult read the words.

- ***How is the child provided feedback, encouragement and reward?***
  Good software makes liberal use of encouragement and rewards. "Fantastic!" and "Let's try that again" are positive feedback. Rewards can take the form of points, money, bonus points, etc. Graphics and sounds are important as well. Fireworks or an animated host saying the words will help keep your child going. Your child should also be given clues to the right answers when an error has been made.

- ***What is the level of difficulty?***
  Make sure the level of difficulty is appropriate. Guidelines are usually printed on the package and are generally accurate. It is important that software allow the child to increase or decrease the level of difficulty during the session. If your child is having difficulties and is unable to go to an easier level, he simply gets frustrated and learns nothing. Equally important is the ability to increase the level of difficulty to encourage learning growth.

- ***How does the software offer help?***
  In software where drill or exercises are the focus, partially or fully solved examples are important. That way, the child does not go into the exercise cold. Regular feedback on specific questions and on the child's progress is also important. Many adventure and simulation software offer hints to allow the child to progress without getting bogged down. Too often, though, these hints just make it very easy to progress without any real learning going on.

- ***Where do I get more information?***
  Better computer software stores allow and even encourage customers to sit down and try the software. This is probably the best way to evaluate potential purchases. There are also many magazines that specialize in home software. They frequently test software using real children as evaluators. Your local school may have ideas on appropriate software or software used by teachers or other families.

Recommended math software

Math Ace (Magic Quest). Ages 8-14.
Math Blaster series (Davidson). Many age-level packages.
Mathville (Courseware Solutions). Three packages: grades 1-3, 4-6, 7-9.
Mighty Math series (Edmark). Many age-level packages.
Reader Rabbit – Math Journey series (The Learning Company). Many grade-level packages.

Recommended full-curriculum software

Jumpstart Grade series (Knowledge Adventure). Many grade-level packages.
Reader Rabbit's Grade series (The Learning Company). Many grade-level packages.

Recommended adventure and problem-solving software

Carmen San Diego series (Broderbund).

Clockwerks (Spectrum HoloByte).

Dr. Brain series (Sierra).

I Spy (Scholastic).

Nightmare Ned (Disney Interactive).

Tetris (Blue Planet Software).

The Incredible Machine series (Sierra).

Trail Adventure series (The Learning Company).

Treasure Mountain (The Learning Company).

Mathematics workbooks

Many parents decide to buy workbooks for their children, hoping they are making the right choice along the way. Speak to your child's teacher for some specific titles he may like, or for ideas on choosing an appropriate workbook for your child. Here are some tips on what to consider when choosing a workbook.

- ***Is the book geared to the appropriate level?***
  A workbook should be labelled as to the grade or age level. Check to see if the language is also appropriate for your child's reading level. Ask him to read a few sentences to see if he understands the language.

- ***Is the workbook topic-specific or does it cover a wide spectrum of concepts?***
  Because a workbook is meant to help your child with specific concepts or skills, it is best to be topic-specific, such as "geometry" or "addition and subtraction". Make sure the workbook deals with the skills in which your child needs help.

- ***How is it laid out?***

  A good workbook will use its layout to keep the interest of the child. Lists and lists of exercises may or may not be a turn-off. One child may respond to them simply because it is not "homework." Others may need pictures and games. The layout should invite the child to want to keep going until the section is finished. However, if it is too fancy and cluttered, it can be distracting and confusing.

- ***How does it teach the skills or concepts?***

  A workbook should use acceptable methods to teach your child the skills or concepts he is struggling with. Solved examples should come with clear and concise explanations. Kids get bored very quickly if the explanations are too wordy. Pictures or graphics enhance learning by making math more concrete.

- ***Are the units of measurement appropriate?***

  Read the material in the workbook to make sure that the units of measurement are appropriate for your child's environment. Kilograms or pounds? $Canadian or $US? Celsius or Fahrenheit? This is a very important consideration.

- ***Are the exercises graduated?***

  Any exercises should begin with fairly easy problems and gradually become more complex in nature. This gives your child early success and allows him to develop more complex skills.

- ***How does it look?***

  Does the book use appealing colors? Does it have an appealing cover? Are the pictures appropriate for your child's age level? Some children will tolerate pictures below their grade level. Others will dislike them.

Recommended workbooks and activity books

Active Minds Workbooks, Chapters. Grades 1-8. Available in 2000.

Building the Basics, by Errol Yeaman, Benchmark Press, 1997. Grade-level series.

Calendar Math, Toronto Board of Education, annually. All grades.

Circles: Shapes in Math, Science and Nature, by Catherine Sheldrick Ross, Kids Can Press, 1994. Grades 4-9.

Discovering Math, by David L. Steinecker, Marshall Cavendish, 1996. Grade-level series.

Even More Mathematical Activities, by Brian Bolt, Cambridge University Press, 1987. All grades.

Family Math, by Jean Kerr Stenmark, Virginia Thompson and Ruth Cossey, Lawrence Hall of Science, 1986. All grades.

Math Sticker Workbooks, Elan Press, 1997. Grade-level series.

Mathematical Activities, by Brian Bolt, Cambridge University Press, 1982. All grades.

Triangles: Shapes in Math, Science and Nature, by Catherine Sheldrick Ross, Kids Can Press, 1994. Grades 4-9.

Recommended math puzzle and game books

Anno's Math Games, by Mitsumasa Anno, Paper Star, 1997. All grades.

Anno's Math Games II, by Mitsumasa Anno, Paper Star, 1997. All grades.

Anno's Math Games III, by Mitsumasa Anno, Paper Star, 1997. All grades.

Entertaining Mathematical Puzzles, by Martin Gardner, Dover, 1986. Grades 4-12.

(and numerous others by Martin Gardner)

Lewis Carroll's Games and Puzzles, by Edward Wakeling (ed.), Dover, 1992. Grades 4-12.

The World's Best Optical Illusions, by Charles H. Paraquin, Sterling, 1987. Grades 4-12.

Some fun books with a mathematics theme

The King's Chessboard, by David Birch, Puffin Pied Piper, 1988. Grades 5-9.

Math Curse, by Jon Scieszka and Lane Smith, Viking, 1995. Grades 7-12.

Games that build math skills

Games are a fun way of building math skills. Some games build these skills through a themed approach, with the math built in to the activities. Others use logic and strategy. Still others use math as the obvious approach. Know what to look for when considering purchasing a game.

- ***Are the rules easy to follow?***
  Make sure the rules are easy to follow, not only for adults, but also for children. Simple, straightforward rules enable a child to play without adult supervision. If the game is too complex, it may turn off your child.

- ***Is it age appropriate?***
  Most games give an appropriate age range on their label. If your child is near the upper end of the range, it may not be worth-while buying it.

- ***Does it build the skills you are looking for?***
  Check to make sure the game develops or reinforces specific skills you are looking for.

- ***Is the theme of interest to your child?***
  It doesn't matter how interesting the game may be to you, make sure the theme is of interest to your child. A high interest level makes the game more fun, longer lasting and probably easier to play.

- ***What type of game play is required?***
  Is the type of play ruled by chance, logic, strategy, problem solving or a combination of them? Good games will involve at least two, if not more, types of game-playing skills.

- ***Where should I buy a game?***
  Department stores carry mostly the traditional favorites. Game, hobby and educational-supply stores will carry a wider variety and math-specific games.

Recommended games that build math skills

Backgammon. Age 8+.

Battleship (Milton Bradley). Age 8+.

Checkers. Age 6+.

Chess. Age 8+.

Chinese Checkers. Age 6+.

Dominoes. Age 6+.

GiGamic (Abalone Games). Age 8+.

Labrynth (Ravensburger). Age 10+.

Life (Milton Bradley). Age 8+.

Mastermind (Chieftain Products). Age 10+.

Mixmath (Wrebbit Inc.). Age 9+.

Monopoly (Parker Brothers). Age 8+.

Pinpoint (Oliver Games). Age 8+.

Pyraos (Abalone Games). Age 8+.

Quads (Abalone Games). Age 8+.

Quarto (Abalone Games). Age 8+.

Quixo (Abalone Games). Age 8+.

Quoridor (Abalone Games). Age 8+.

Ready or Not (Cottage Canada Games). Age 9+.

Rubiks Cube (Sevens Towns). Age 9+.

Rubiks Magic (Sevens Towns). Age 9+.

Rubiks Snake (Sevens Towns). Age 9+.

Rubiks Tangle (Sevens Towns). Age 9+.

Rubiks Triamid (Sevens Towns). Age 9+.

Set (Set Enterprises). Age 6+.

Tangoes (Rex Games). Age 8+.

Wire Puzzles (Puzzle Master). Age 8+.

CHAPTER THIRTEEN

Ten math puzzlers

1. A Logical Race (Age 9+)

Mary, Kathy, Laurie, Jenna and Fei ran in a race. There were no ties.

Mary did not come in last, but Jenna finished before her.

Kathy was not in fourth place.

Laurie did not do better than Fei.

Laurie came in before Jenna.

Fei did better than Jenna.

In what position did each of the girls finish?

2. Six Faces of a Cube (Age 9+)

Four different views of a cube are shown. What is the picture on the missing face of the fourth view?

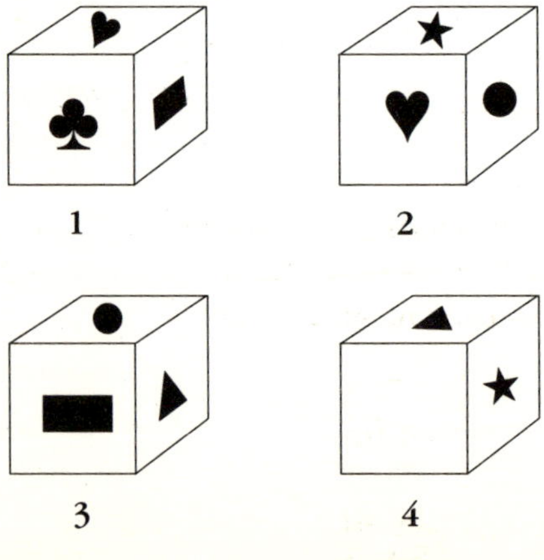

3. Toothpick Squares (Age 8+)

There are 12 toothpicks in the diagram below. Take 2 toothpicks away so you are left with only 2 squares.

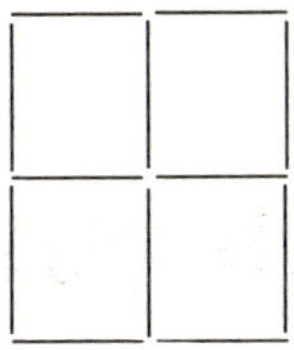

4. Pick a Number (Age 12+)

Pick any number.

Double the number.

Add 6.

Divide by 2.

Subtract the original number.

Your answer is 3.

Why?

5. Magic Squares (Age 8+)

In a magic square, the numbers in each row, column and diagonal add up to the same number. This number is known as the magic sum.

Use all the numbers from 1 to 9 in (a) with a magic sum of 15.

Use all the numbers from 1 to 16 in (b) with a magic sum of 34.

(a)

	1	

(b)

1			

6. Multiplication Teaser (Age 11+)

Each letter represents a different prime number less than 10. What does each number equal?

$$\begin{array}{r} 7a5 \\ \underline{\times\ b3} \\ 2bc5 \\ \underline{c32d0} \\ 25da5 \end{array}$$

7. *One to Four (Age 10+)*

Place +, −, × or ÷ symbols between 1, 2, 3 and 4, in any order to get each number from 0 to 15 as an answer. One of them is already done for you. Make sure you follow the proper order of operations.

$$2 \times 4 - 3 + 1 = 6$$

8. *Number Circles (Age 9+)*

Follow the number patterns in the circles to find the missing number.

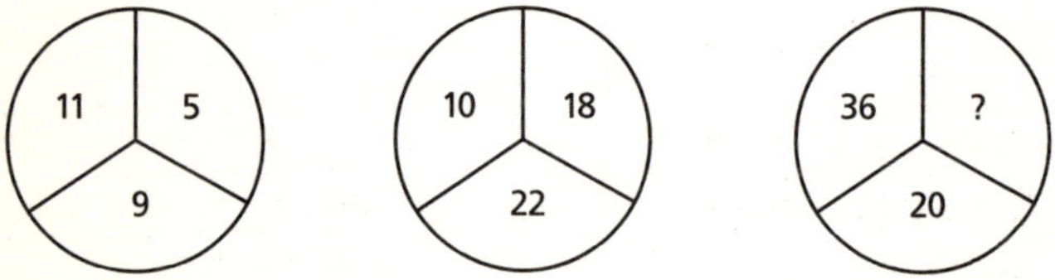

9. *Mathematical Sentences (Age 10+)*

Fill in the blanks with ( ), +, −, × or ÷ to make each number sentence true.

$$5 \quad 5 \quad 5 \quad 5 = 3$$

$$4 \quad 4 \quad 4 \quad 4 = 8$$

$$3 \quad 3 \quad 3 \quad 3 = 4$$

10. *A Family of Seven (Age 12+)*

The Browns have seven children – Jamie, Eric, Vanessa, Dave, Pete, Amanda and Kim. All children are different ages and are between 1 and 18 years old. Jamie is twice Eric's age. Dave's age is the same as Eric's and Amanda's combined. Amanda is 1 year older than Kim's digits added together. Kim is 10 years older than Eric. Vanessa and Pete are 2 years apart. Eric is 8 years younger than Dave. Pete is 5 years younger than Kim. Vanessa's age is a multiple of 3. How old is each child?

SOLUTIONS TO MATH PUZZLERS

1. 1st - Fei
   2nd - Laurie
   3rd - Jenna
   4th - Mary
   5th - Kathy

2. 

3. 

4. Let the number be ■.

Double the number.	2■
Add 6.	2■+6
Divide by 2.	■+3
Subtract the original number.	3
Your answer is 3.	

5. (a)

8	1	6
3	5	7
4	9	2

(b)

1	12	7	14
8	13	2	11
10	3	16	5
15	6	9	4

6. a=7 b=3
   c=2 d=5

7.

$4-3-2+1=0$	$3+4+2-1=8$
$2\times3-4-1=1$	$3\times4-2-1=9$
$4-3+2-1=2$	$1+2+3+4=10$
$1\times4-3+2=3$	$3\times4-2+1=11$
$2\times4-3-1=4$	$2\times4+3+1=12$
$2\times4-3\times1=5$	$3\times4+2-1=13$
$2\times4-3+1=6$	$4\times3\times1+2=14$
$3\times4\div2+1=7$	$3\times4+2+1=15$

8.

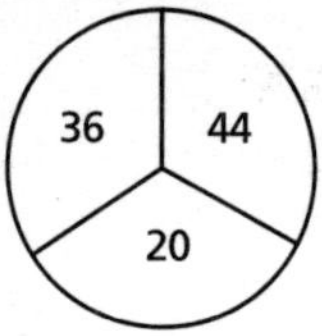

9. $(5+5+5)\div5=3$
$4\times4-4-4=8$
$(3\times3+3)\div3=4$

10. Eric - 6
Amanda - 8
Vanessa - 9
Pete - 11
Jamie - 12
Dave - 14
Kim - 16

CHAPTER FOURTEEN

Five math games for the family

1. A Mathematical walk (All ages)

Required materials

paper and pencil

Take a mathematical walk around the neighborhood. As you're walking, look for anything mathematical. Suggested items to look for:

- triangles (e.g., rooflines)
- circles (e.g., wheels)
- other geometric shapes (e.g., street signs)
- decimal numbers (e.g., prices)
- percents (e.g., store sales)
- parallel lines (e.g., sidewalks)
- statistics (e.g., advertising)
- 3-D solids (e.g., buildings)
- volume (e.g., packaging)
- speed (e.g., speedometer)

Record each item, describing how each is used. Older children can make up mathematical problems involving the item. This could evolve into a school project by taking a camera along, shooting pictures and making a poster of math around us.

2. Double Dice Game (Age 8+)

Required materials

Four dice of two different colors, paper and pencil

Object of the game

To roll more different products than anyone else.

Play

- The first player rolls the 4 dice (say 2 red and 2 white). Add the 2 white dice together and the 2 red dice together. Then multiply the 2 numbers together. Record the final product.
- Each player, in turn, repeats the play.
- Continue until each player has rolled 15 times (or any agreed-upon total).
- If a player has already recorded the product on his or her own sheet, no re-roll is permitted.
- The winner is the player that has rolled the most *different* products.

3. License-Plate Patterns (Age 9+)

Required materials

None

When driving on the highway, play a game in which mathematical patterns on license plates are discovered by the family members. The patterns can be developed by adding (135), subtracting (963), multiplying (248), dividing (421), letter patterns (ABC), words with numbers (ONE 111), palindromes (12321) or any mathematical patterns. Older children may have an advantage, so you could take turns or restrict their types of patterns to more difficult ones. This can be simply a fun game. There need not be a winner.

4. Integer Darts (Age 11+)

Required materials

Dart board, four darts, paper and pencil or chalkboard

Play a standard game of darts, except on odd-numbered throws, add the points to your own score. On even-numbered throws, subtract the points from your opponent's score. If there are more than two players, you could subtract from the player immediately after you. If a score drops below zero, it become negative or "in the hole," and must get back to zero before becoming positive again. The winner is the first to reach 100. This adds a lot of laughter to the game and helps improve integer skills.

5. Card Scrabble (Age 8+)

Required materials

Two decks of cards for up to three players or three decks of cards for more players; paper and pencil

Object of the game

To produce mathematical patterns (using +, −, × or ÷) with playing cards in a Scrabble format.

Play

Shuffle the cards well. Keep the Jokers in the deck. They are to be used as wild cards. Deal seven cards face-down to each player.

- Start with one card face-up on the table.
- The first player lays down at least two more cards to form a mathematical pattern. The player receives one point for each card used. This player retrieves an equal number of cards from the deck to replace the cards used.
- The play rotates clockwise. Each player must form a pattern consisting of three or more cards and must build on to the existing cards. If a player extends a pattern, points are granted only for the extra cards used.

Notes

A=1, J=12, Q=15, K=20.

Joker is wild and can take the place of any card.

Alternate rules

Toughen the game by making a rule that all cards must be of the same suit or color, or all different suits or alternating suits. Points could also be granted by the face value of the cards.

APPENDIX

What your child should know, by grade level

The following information is a general guide of what your child is normally expected to be able to do in math at the end of each grade level from grade 3 to 7. They are taken from the Ontario and British Columbia standards and will apply to most Canadian jurisdictions. However, content will vary somewhat classroom by classroom, school by school, district by district and province by province. For more detailed information on your local standards, contact your child's school.

NUMBER FACTS AND CALCULATIONS

GRADE 3

- Read and print numerals to 1000 and words to 100.
- Represent numbers with pictures and objects.
- Addition and subtraction of 3-digit whole numbers.
- Know multiplication and division facts of 1-digit whole numbers to 7×7.
- Identify numbers divisible by 2, 5 and 10.
- Represent simple fractions using pictures or objects.
- Solve problems involving more than one operation.
- Justify reasons for the problem-solving method chosen.

GRADE 4

- Read and write whole numbers to 10,000.
- Read, compare and order 2-decimal numbers.
- Understand decimals as tenths, hundredths, etc. and represent them using pictures and objects.

- Know multiplication and division facts of 1-digit whole numbers to 9×9.
- Addition and subtraction of 4-digit whole numbers.
- Multiplication and division of a 3-digit by a 1-digit whole number.
- Addition and subtraction of decimal numbers to 1 decimal place.
- Read, compare and order simple proper and improper fractions with common denominators.
- Solve problems involving whole numbers and decimals, with and without a calculator.
- Justify reasons for the problem-solving method chosen.

GRADE 5

- Addition of three 4-digit numbers.
- Subtraction of two 4-digit numbers.
- Multiplication of two 2-digit numbers.
- Division of a 4-digit by a 1-digit number.
- Represent, compare and order whole numbers, decimals and fractions using pictures, objects and number lines.
- Know multiplication and division facts of whole numbers to 12×12.
- Addition and subtraction of decimals to 2 decimal places.
- Multiplication and division of 1-digit whole numbers by decimal numbers to 2 decimal places.
- Demonstrate the equivalence of simple fractions (e.g., $\frac{2}{4}=\frac{1}{2}$).
- Solve and pose 2-step problems involving whole numbers and decimals, with and without a calculator.
- Justify their reasoning for the operations chosen when problem solving involves decimals and fractions.

GRADE 6

- Recognize, read and write whole numbers to 1,000,000 and decimal numbers to 3 decimal places.
- Compare and order common and mixed fractions with unlike denominators, using diagrams, objects and number lines.

- Column addition with 3-digit whole numbers.
- Subtraction of 5-digit whole numbers.
- Multiplication of a 3-digit with a 2-digit whole number.
- Division of a 4-digit by a 2-digit whole number.
- Addition and subtraction of decimal numbers to 3 decimal places.
- Multiplication and division of 1-digit whole numbers with decimal numbers to 3 decimal places.
- Use the correct order of operations with whole number sentences.
- Understand fractions as related to percents, ratios, decimals, etc.
- Calculate simple percents.
- Begin to identify the use of integers in temperature, money, etc.
- Solve and pose problems involving whole numbers, fractions, decimals, percents, rate and ratios, with and without a calculator.
- Justify their reasoning when solving problems involving whole numbers, fractions, decimals and percents.

GRADE 7

- Compare and order integers, decimals, multiples, factors and square roots.
- Understand that exponents represent repeated multiplication.
- Add and subtract simple fractions.
- Multiply a fraction with a whole number.
- Understand the order of operations including brackets.
- Add and subtract integers.
- Convert between fractions, decimals and percents.
- Pose and solve problems involving integers, decimals, fractions and percents.

MEASUREMENT

GRADE 3

- Estimate, measure, record, compare and order linear measurements in standard units (centimetres, decimetres, metres and kilometres).

- Measure perimeter using standard units.
- Estimate and measure area using uniform non-standard units (given shapes).
- Estimate and measure the capacity of containers using standard units (millilitre, litre).
- Estimate and measure the mass of objects using standard units (gram, kilogram).
- Read and write time to the nearest minute using a digital clock and to the nearest 5 minutes using an analog clock.
- Estimate and measure the passage of time in minutes, days, weeks, months and years.
- Estimate, read and record temperature in degrees Celsius.
- Make purchases and change up to $10.
- Write money in both cents and dollar notation.
- Solve problems involving measurement and estimation.

GRADE 4

- Understand the relation between mm, cm, m and km.
- Draw items of a given length.
- Select the appropriate unit of linear, area, mass and volume measurement.
- Use precision to measure length, perimeter and area.
- Estimate the area of regular polygons using 1 cm square grid paper.
- Understand that two objects of different shape can have the same perimeter or area.
- Use blocks to model three-dimensional figures.
- Understand the relation between grams and kilograms.
- Understand the relation between years, decades, centuries and millenniums.
- Understand money purchases and relations up to $50.
- Solve problems involving length, perimeter, area, mass, volume, time and money.

GRADE 5

- Full understanding of linear measurement and metric units and prefixes.

- Develop rules and formulas for the perimeter and area of a rectangle.
- Estimate and calculate the perimeter and area of rectangles and squares.
- Use grid paper to estimate the area of irregular polygons.
- Use standard units to measure volumes of containers.
- Determine the relationship between volume and capacity through displacement of a liquid.
- Understand the relationship between millilitres and cubic centimetres and between kilograms and tonnes.
- Use appropriate units of measurement for volume and mass.
- Begin to understand the speed relationship between distance and time.
- Read and write dates using SI notation (1999 02 28).
- Read and write time to the nearest second.
- Estimate and measure time to the nearest second.
- Read, write and estimate money values to $1000 and make change to $100.

GRADE 6

- Understand the relationship between linear, square and cubic units of measurement.
- Understand the area relation for a rectangle: area=length×width.
- Understand the area relationships between rectangles, squares, parallelograms and triangles.
- Calculate the area of a rectangle, square, parallelogram and triangle.
- Sketch a rectangle, square, triangle or parallelogram, given its area or perimeter.
- Determine the rules for calculating the volume of a rectangular prism (box).
- Estimate and calculate the volume of a rectangular prism.
- Understand the relationship between milligrams, grams and kilograms.
- Use appropriate metric units when solving problems in length, area, volume, capacity and mass.

- Make simple metric conversions.
- Read, write, estimate and count money values to $10,000.

GRADE 7

- Research and report on commonly used measurement instruments.
- Describe and define measurement concepts using appropriate vocabulary.
- Find the area of irregular shapes by breaking them into simple shapes.
- Estimate the area and perimeter of irregular shapes.
- Develop and use formulas for the areas of parallelograms and trapezoids.
- Develop and use formulas for the circumference of a circle.
- Use nets to develop the surface area formula for a rectangular prism.
- Develop and use the formula for the volume of a rectangular prism.

GEOMETRY

GRADE 3

- Compare and sort two- and three-dimensional shapes according to their attributes.
- Build rectangular prisms (boxes) from given nets (line drawings).
- Use a variety of two- and three-dimensional building materials to build three-dimensional models and describe the process.
- Sketch three-dimensional models.
- Identify congruent two- and three-dimensional shapes.
- Identify typical two-dimensional shapes (square, rectangle, parallelogram, rhombus).
- Solve geometric puzzles in two-dimensions.
- Understand lines of symmetry for two-dimensional shapes.
- Identify and perform transformations such as flips, slides and turns.
- Describe movement on a grid.

GRADE 4

- Identify and sort two-dimensional figures (triangles, squares, parallelograms, trapezoids, etc.).
- Identify and sketch two-dimensional faces on three-dimensional figures.
- Design and build three-dimensional figures using toothpicks, straws, etc.
- Construct two- and three-dimensional congruent figures.
- Identify geometric patterns.
- Use a protractor to measure angles.
- Solve problems involving geometric properties and concepts in the everyday world.
- Find and draw lines of symmetry.
- Solve problems involving flips, slides and turns using concrete materials.
- Identify transformational patterns.
- Use a coordinate system (grid) in simple games (Battleship).

GRADE 5

- Identify and construct nets of cubes and pyramids.
- Sort polygons by number of sides, angles and vertices.
- Classify polygons by angle and side properties.
- Show congruence using such techniques as transformations and paper folding.
- Use a variety of tools to construct triangles given specific measures of angles and sides.
- Measure and construct angles using a protractor.
- Understand and apply translations, reflections, rotations and tiling patterns.
- Construct shapes with a single line of symmetry.
- Apply coordinate systems on grids and maps.

GRADE 6

- Use grid and isometric dot paper to design nets of cubes and pyramids and build them using interlocking cubes.
- Sketch nets of three-dimensional figures.
- Sort polygons by lines of symmetry and rotational symmetry.

- Understand congruent and similar figures.
- Estimate sizes of angles.
- Construct two-dimensional shapes with more than one line of symmetry.
- Construct two-dimensional shapes given specific angle and side measures.
- Analyze the effects of translations, rotations and reflections.
- Construct tiling patterns to cover a plane.
- Plot positive points in a Cartesian plane (grid).

GRADE 7

- Recognize and sketch the front, side and top view of three-dimensional objects.
- Build three-dimensional objects from nets.
- Identify congruent two-dimensional shapes, providing reasons for their congruency.
- Create and describe designs made from translations, rotations and reflections of two-dimensional shapes, with and without a computer.
- Determine whether a shape will tile a plane.

PATTERNING AND ALGEBRA

Before grade 7, patterning is rarely taught as a topic by itself. It is generally used as a technique for understanding concepts in number operations, measurement and geometry. Beginning in grade 7, patterning is linked with algebra and becomes much more abstract in its concepts.

GRADE 3

- Identify and extend patterns in involving two or more attributes (e.g., shape, color).
- Create patterns involving two or more attributes.
- Identify pattern relationships involving addition, subtraction, multiplication and division.
- Create models involving environmental patterns (e.g., weather).
- Display patterns in chart form.

GRADE 4

- Recognize mathematical relationships in patterns.
- Describe and solve problems involving patterns in real life (e.g., money, architecture, quilts).
- Analyze number patterns and generalize with a rule.
- Given a rule, extend the pattern.
- Determine a missing term in an addition or subtraction pattern.

GRADE 5

- Recognize and discuss the relationship between a term's value and its position (e.g., term 1=5, term 2=8, etc.).
- Understand patterns that involve two alternating changes (e.g., add 3 then add 5).
- Describe, model and extend patterns in any meaningful context (e.g., games).
- Create charts to summarize patterns and to make predictions based on the results.

GRADE 6

- Recognize more complex pattern relationships involving addition, subtraction, multiplication and division and generalize them (e.g., doubling each term to get the next; adding 3 then multiplying by 3).
- Create charts and graphs to summarize patterns.
- Given a rule expressed in mathematical language, extend the pattern.
- Given a set of data summarized in a table of values, state a rule and graph the data.
- Pose and solve problems involving mathematical patterns.

GRADE 7

- Identify patterns, extend them by completing a table.
- Use patterns to make predictions.
- Understand that a variable represents a set of numbers.
- Evaluate simple equations (e.g., $x+3=5$, $3x=15$, $2x+1=7$)

by substitution and trial and error with results being whole numbers.

- Translate statements into algebraic expressions.

STATISTICS AND CHANCE

GRADE 3

- Sort objects using two or more attributes (e.g., size, color).
- Classify and organize objects and data using charts and Venn diagrams.
- Design a survey containing questions requiring a finite number of responses.
- Construct bar graphs and pictographs using scales with multiples of 1, 2, 5 and 10.
- Interpret data from bar graphs, pictographs, circle graphs and Venn diagrams.
- Understand many-to-one correspondences in pictographs (1 horse represents 10 horses).
- Conduct simple probability experiments using spinners and dice and predict the results.
- Predict the probability that an event will occur.

GRADE 4

- Find examples of data in the real world.
- Conduct a survey, record the data on a tally sheet and summarize using bar graphs.
- Predict the possible results of a survey.
- Analyze data by explaining the results and determining the range of the data.
- Interpret data from charts, tables and graphs, discussing the important features.
- Construct bar graphs by hand and by computer.
- Use proper labelling: title, labels, axes, intervals, data points.
- Understand the meaning of a fraction of a picture in a pictograph.
- Conduct probability experiments, making decisions based on the results.

- Compare predicted results of a probability experiment with the actual results.
- Use tree diagrams to organize data, based on probabilities.

GRADE 5

- Design surveys, collect the data, record the results on a spreadsheet or tally sheet and display the data on graphs (line graphs, bar graphs, pictographs, circle graphs) by hand and by computer, labelling fully.
- Analyze how the data were collected and the reasonableness of the results.
- Analyze data, tables, charts and graphs and use the information in discussions.
- Calculate the mean and mode of a set of numeric data.
- Recognize bias in graphs, charts and tables.
- Use fractions to express probability.
- Use tree diagrams to display the results of a probability experiment.
- Connect real-life situations with probability (1 out of 10 people).

GRADE 6

- Organize data into self-selected categories.
- Select the type of graph that best represents the data in a survey.
- Evaluate how data were collected and how the results represent a population.
- Understand how the choice of intervals affects how data appear in a graph.
- Calculate the mean of a set of numeric data.
- Construct line graphs and scatter plots by hand and computer.
- Analyze data and convincingly use the results in an argument.
- Connect the probability of an event with the number of possible outcomes (e.g., when tossing a coin, the probability of a head is $\frac{1}{2}$ because there are 2 sides).
- Understand the independence of trials (e.g., one coin toss does not affect the next).

- Compare experimental results with probabilities based on theory (e.g., results after 10 coin tosses).

***GRADE* 7**

- Collect and organize data using tally charts, frequency tables and stem-and-leaf diagrams.
- Use spreadsheets and databases to record and retrieve data and to do research.
- Display data on bar graphs, pictographs and circle graphs, with and without a computer, labelling properly.
- Calculate the measures of central tendency (mean, median and mode) of a set of numeric data.
- Understand the different meanings of mean, median and mode.
- Analyze a set of data, using measures of central tendency, graphs and words.
- Describe trends in graphs and make predictions.
- Use the results of data analysis to make convincing arguments.

Sources:

Ontario Ministry of Education and Training (1997 standards)
British Columbia Ministry of Education (1996 standards)

NOTES & UPDATES